Dave -
So sorry it
took so long
to get ... you.

A

No Place Like Home

Angel Power

One Printers Way
Altona, MB R0G 0B0
Canada

www.friesenpress.com

Copyright © 2022 by Angel Power
First Edition — 2022

ISBN
978-1-03-915134-5 (Hardcover)
978-1-03-915133-8 (Paperback)
978-1-03-915135-2 (eBook)

1. FICTION, PSYCHOLOGICAL

Distributed to the trade by The Ingram Book Company

No Place Like Home

Chapter 1

THE BRAKES OF THE MOVING van hissed as it pulled to a stop in front of a white bungalow with green trim. Crystal sat in the passenger seat of her Uncle Frank's battered red Toyota as they pulled in behind the truck. She hopped out of the car, stretched, and looked around. The house from the outside was not bad. They had lived in worse. The driveway was gravel and led along the side of the house to a door.

There were two small windows in the front on one end, and a large bow window on the other, overlooking the front lawn. The paint was faded and needed attention. There were remnants of a flower garden under the bow window and a lot of shrubs. It wouldn't take long to get the shrubbery trimmed and the flower garden growing again.

Crystal turned and watched her Uncle Frank climb out of the car. He was an attractive man in his mid-forties and was average height and weight. His hair was beginning to turn salt and peppery, but he hid the signs of aging well.

"What do you think, Crystal?" he asked.

"It's nice. We'll mow the lawn, trim the shrubs, replace the flowers, and touch up the paint. It'll look great."

"I'm sorry about Pembroke. This town will be different, I promise."

"Sure, Uncle Frank."

It was the same promise every time. Then, it wasn't long before they were moving on to another town. Uncle Frank went to speak to the movers, and Crystal walked around to the back. There was a nice fenced-in area with a few patio stones placed together, surrounding the steps leading from the back door.

Crystal looked over the fence into the neighbour's backyard. There was a sand box, swing set, and jungle gym. There would be children living there. The screen door suddenly swung open and out bounced a dark-haired little girl. She dashed to the jungle gym and swung herself onto the platform.

"Katie, be careful. You'll hurt yourself," a masculine voice yelled from the window.

When the little girl noticed Crystal watching her, she stopped, jumped down, and ran to the fence.

"Who are you?" she asked, her eyes wide and full of curiosity.

"I'm Crystal Pearson, your new neighbour."

"I'm Katie Blackburn, and I'm seven. How old are you? Can we be friends?" she asked quickly.

"I'm twenty-three. I'd like that," Crystal said smiling.

Katie's hair was chestnut brown, wavy, and cropped

short. Her deep brown eyes were accentuated with long, full lashes. Her dazzling smile revealed a mischievous little girl. Crystal looked up as a shadow swiftly approached, moving across the lawn.

"This is my dad, Michael. Dad, this is Crystal, our new neighbour," Katie said, turning towards the man.

"Hi, nice to meet you," Crystal said shyly, looking into the most exquisite blue eyes she had ever seen. "You moving in?" he asked, eyeing her carefully.

"Yes, we're coming from Pembroke, Ontario. My uncle found a job at the mill," she replied, trying to recover her composure.

Before Michael could reply, a man's voice came from the front of the house.

"Crystal, the movers want to know where you want things," Uncle Frank yelled.

"Gotta run," Crystal said, turning towards the voice.

What a neighbour! she thought as she looked back and waved to Michael and Katie before disappearing.

Crystal spoke to the movers and went into the house. She looked at herself in the bathroom mirror. She was far from cover-girl beautiful, but she was no plain Jane either. Her straight, long, dirty-blonde hair hung loosely over her shoulders to the small of her back. Her clothes were wrinkled from the long trip. But they perfectly fit her slender five-foot-eight-inch frame.

As she leaned closer to the mirror, her dark eyes looked like small black marbles lying in red pools from three days of straight driving and a lack of sleep from the overnight Marine Atlantic ferry crossing. She hardly ever wore makeup.

Without it, she was still an attractive young woman, that is, when she was rested and not on the move.

Crystal left the bathroom and went into the kitchen to begin unpacking. This was the worst thing about moving, all the packing and unpacking. They had just gotten the last place straightened away when they were packing up and moving again. She hoped things would be different here in Corner Brook, but she never knew when Uncle Frank would come home to announce they were moving again.

Crystal watched Michael through the window above the sink. He was crawling around the ground with Katie on his back. Michael bucked like a horse, and Katie would slide off onto the grass laughing. My childhood was so different, she thought.

Frank was her mother's brother. When Crystal was four, her parents had died in a car crash, and she had gone to live with him. She couldn't remember her parents, and there were no pictures of them. Uncle Frank assured her she looked exactly like her mother. He didn't attend the funeral. They had moved immediately because of Uncle Frank's grief over the death of his sister.

Her parents were poor and had few belongings. Uncle Frank gave everything her parents had owned to charity. The house they lived in was rented, and after the funeral expenses were paid there was nothing left. Uncle Frank was her only living relative, and he had agreed to take Crystal in.

Crystal had always been grateful to him for taking on the responsibility of a little girl, and she realized Uncle Frank tried to do the best he could for her. It was because of Uncle Frank's drinking problem that they moved so much. When he first went to Alcoholics Anonymous, things had been wonderful for a while, but being jilted by Rosie two towns ago had sent him whirling into a drinking binge and had cost him his job, so they had moved to Pembroke.

Pembroke had been fine, too, before the drinking started again. Crystal didn't know what triggered his drinking binges. There were times when she wanted to move out, but she couldn't leave her uncle alone. He had saved her from a life in an orphanage. She felt she owed him.

They had lived in so many different places while she was growing up that she had lost track. When she was young, they were moving all the time, about every four to six months. As she grew older, the moves slowed down. Uncle Frank drank less and kept his jobs longer.

Crystal stood gazing out the window, wondering how long they would be here. The job at the mill sounded like a good one. She prayed Uncle Frank would control his drinking. Her thoughts turned to the man playing with his little girl.

Michael was tall and athletic, with short black hair. He had wide, strong-looking shoulders, and the outline of rippling biceps strained against the short sleeves of his t-shirt. His skin was lightly bronzed from long hours in the sun. He had full, sensuous lips and a warm, inviting smile that accented the clean, chiseled features of his face.

"You won't get anything done staring out the window. The movers have finished unloading. I'm going to the mill to meet the supervisor and see about this job." Uncle Frank's gruff voice made her jump as the front door slammed behind him on his way out.

Crystal finished unpacking the kitchen boxes, straightened up and stood back to take a look. The paint was white, so you could do anything with it. Some pictures added to the walls, bright curtains and a few odds and ends would dress it up nicely. She took a steak from the fridge, tossed a salad, and sliced a fresh baguette. Then she went out the back door to start the barbecue to grill her steak.

"It's a great night to barbecue, isn't it?" Michael called over the fence. "Katie loves hotdogs. It's hard to get her to eat anything else. I'll have to stop buying them, so she'll be forced to eat something different. I usually wait until she's in bed to have my meal."

"You're welcome to join me. Uncle Frank went to the mill and hasn't come back yet. He probably got tied up."

Michael glanced at his watch. "There wouldn't be anyone there this late. The mill shuts down by six."

"Maybe he ran into someone he knows. We've moved around a lot."

"My steak is done. I'll be right over," Michael said.

Crystal turned her steak over and went inside to gather the utensils to set the patio table. Michael appeared carrying a plate loaded with vegetables, a steak, and a baked potato.

"It's nice having company during a meal for a change," Crystal said smiling. "Uncle Frank is always late. Most of the time, I eat alone."

"Where did you say you moved from?" Michael asked, pulling up a chair and sitting down.

"We came from Pembroke, Ontario. We've moved around a lot," Crystal replied, and gave him a brief description of some of the towns and cities they'd lived in.

"You must have found it difficult during your school years," he remarked.

"No, not really. We moved so much I didn't have time to make friends. It gave me mountains of time to study. I did well, actually."

"Did you date?"

"No. Uncle Frank didn't like me bringing friends home, male or female."

The crunch of tires on gravel could be heard in the driveway.

"Uncle Frank must be back."

"Crystal! Crystal honey, help me!" Uncle Frank called.

"Coming, Uncle Frank!" Crystal called back, getting up, and heading towards the front of the house.

Uncle Frank sat half in and half out of a cab, his head in his hands. It was easy to see he was drunk. Crystal guided his arm over her shoulder and helped him out of the car. He groaned as he rested his full weight against her. Crystal paid the cab driver and slowly guided her uncle towards the house.

"I'm so sorry," he kept moaning over and over.

"Here, let me help you," Michael said, from behind her.

"That's okay, I can manage this alone," Crystal replied, embarrassed.

"You don't have to when I'm here."

Michael helped Crystal guide her uncle up the stairs and into the house and dropped him onto his bed.

"I hate it when he drinks. Thanks for the help and the company."

"No problem. That's what neighbours are for. Good

night, Crystal."

"Good night, Michael."

The next day, Uncle Frank was up and gone by the time Crystal had climbed out of bed. She made herself a pot of coffee and went outside to contemplate the events of the previous evening.

I think I'm going to like it here, she thought as she enjoyed the sun's warmth before going back inside to finish unpacking.

It was a couple of weeks before Crystal saw Michael and Katie again. She had been busy getting unpacked and settled in. Michael's house was quiet most of the time. She hadn't seen a woman, and neither Michael nor Katie had mentioned one. She knew she had to start looking for a job and decided to do so that morning.

Michael and Katie came out of the back door, and the noise caught her attention.

"How are things this morning? Settling in okay?" he asked.

"Fine, thanks. I thought I'd relax a little before I start looking for a job. I can't sit around all day doing nothing."

"There's not much available in this town aside from working at the mill. Could I interest you in looking after Katie for me until you find something? Katie's sitter had to leave last week. It would certainly help me out until I can find a replacement."

"Sure. I haven't been outside much since we moved in. She can show me around town," Crystal replied. "What do you say, Katie?" she asked, looking at the little girl.

"That would be fun. Can we visit you at the station, Dad?"

"Not today, sweetheart. I'll be in court all day. Maybe tomorrow."

"Are you a cop?" Crystal asked.

"Yes, plainclothes for the town police. Does that make a difference?"

"No, no. It's just that Uncle Frank gets nervous around cops," Crystal quickly replied.

"I won't tell him if you don't," Michael said, winking at her.

"He won't hear it from me," she said, with a little laugh.

"Here's the key to my house. I'll be home at about five. Don't let her get the best of you. If you need anything, call the station. Katie knows the number. You girls have a good day. I'll see you later," Michael said as he climbed into his car.

"Bye, Dad," Katie called after him, waving.

"Well, Katie, it's just you and me. What do you want to do?" Crystal asked looking down at her.

"Can we go to the park playground down the street, and then go for ice cream?"

"The playground and ice cream it is," Crystal replied, taking her hand and leading her towards the park.

When Katie had tired of the monkey bars and swings, they made their way to the ice cream shop. They browsed the shop windows and stopped to visit some puppies playing on the front lawn of a house they were walking by.

"I love dogs, but Uncle Frank says that the way we move, a dog would be too much trouble."

"Dad says he's not home enough to have a dog, but we can get one when I'm old enough to look after it myself. We have an aquarium in the living room. I like feeding the fish."

"Fish are nice. I like them, too. It's relaxing watching them swim around the tank."

"Do you have a mother?" Katie asked suddenly.

"No, my mother and father died in a car accident when I was little. I live with my Uncle Frank."

"My mother died, too. I miss her a lot. Do you miss your mother?"

"Yes, all the time."

After they'd finished their ice cream, they stopped at the corner store and bought a bag of breadcrumbs to feed to the ducks in the pond on their way back to the house.

"Do you want to see a picture of my mother?" Katie asked, as she opened the door and stepped over the threshold.

"Yes, I do," Crystal replied, following her down the hallway to the living room.

Katie handed her a picture in a brass frame. A woman with eyes and facial features identical to Katie's stared back from behind the glass.

"She was very beautiful," Crystal said.

"Dad says I look just like her."

"Your dad is right. You do."

Crystal looked around the living room. It was furnished in beige and brown. There was a stone fireplace along one wall, and another wall held pictures from family vacations. An aquarium bubbled softly under the pictures. The sofa looked like Italian leather, and a Persian rug partially covered the hardwood floor. Suddenly, Michael entered the living room while Crystal stood there holding the picture. She placed it carefully back on the mantel as a sad expression clouded his eyes.

"Katie wanted to show me her mother," Crystal stammered.

"She was a beautiful woman. It's been about two years since she passed away. Katie was five."

"Do you want to stay for dinner?" Katie blurted out.

"It's fine with me," Michael said, obviously thankful for the interruption.

"I guess I'm outnumbered. I'll go home, clean up and be back shortly. Can I bring anything?"

"No, how about we go to the diner? That way Katie will eat something other than hot dogs," Michael replied, with a chuckle.

Crystal went home to take a quick shower. As the hot water streamed over her body, she thought about her new neighbour. Michael was a plainclothes police officer and a widower. He didn't look any more than thirty. The pain in his eyes when he discussed his late wife told Crystal that he had loved her very much.

Crystal stepped out of the shower and dried herself off. She decided on a simple cobalt blue sundress and braided her hair. She searched her closet and pulled out a pair of white leather sandals and lightly brushed on a bit of makeup. After double-checking her appearance in the mirror, she grabbed her purse and hurried next door.

Michael and Katie were waiting in the car. She slid in front beside Michael, and he backed out of the driveway and onto the street. The radio played as they drove towards the diner at the other end of town. Katie spent the trip pointing out what she thought were important landmarks along the way. Michael pulled to a stop in front of the diner, and they went inside.

The waitress smiled and found them a booth in the back. Michael told her about the area, and Katie added details whenever she thought it necessary.

"Tell me more about yourself. How old are you?" Michael asked.

"I'm twenty-three, born in July. I'll be twenty-four this year. You ask a lot of questions."

"Habit of the job. I'm sorry if it makes you feel uncomfortable."

"What about you?" Crystal looked at him with a twinkle in her eyes.

"I'll be thirty-two this September. I'm starting to get old," he laughed.

Katie began to yawn as she tried to make her way through her ice cream sundae.

"We'd better get her home and into bed," Crystal said, gathering Katie's things.

When they arrived back at the house, Michael lifted Katie's limp, sleeping body from the back seat, and carried her towards the door.

"Thank you for a fun time and lovely evening. See you in the morning," Crystal whispered, closing the door behind them.

The days melted together as Michael and Crystal continued to spend time together. They took Katie canoeing, on picnics and to the beach. In the evenings, they sat in Michael's living room or outside in the yard, sipping wine and talking about how Crystal had survived a life with her

Uncle Frank and why she stayed with him. Uncle Frank was going to AA again and living with him was more tolerable than it had been in a long time. He had met someone and was spending his time with her.

Michael talked about how hard it had been managing both a career and Katie on his own after the death of his wife. He'd had a tough time adjusting to living by himself and being both a father and a mother to Katie. He described working with teens on the street and how frustrating it could be, but stressed the rewards of seeing runaways or missing children reunited with their families.

They laughed about things Katie had said or done and shared each other's hopes and dreams. Crystal knew more than a friendship was developing for her, and she hoped Michael might be feeling the same way.

Chapter 2

CORNER BROOK, NEWFOUNDLAND WAS TURNING out to be one of the best places Crystal could remember living in a long time, until one night Uncle Frank didn't come home. Crystal called his girlfriend Gloria. He hadn't stayed with her before, but their relationship was getting serious, so maybe he was going to start.

"Hello, Gloria? This is Crystal, Frank's niece. I was wondering if...?"

"Oh, Crystal," Gloria cut in sounding distraught. "I've not seen or heard from him since he left here the night before last. He usually comes here for supper after work, but he didn't show up last night. I thought he might have gone out with friends, so I called them. Roddy said a man picked him up at work yesterday, and they drove away. I was going to wait to see if he would call me this morning before calling you. What could've happened to him?"

"I don't know, but I know someone who can help," Crystal replied with a worried tone. "Call me if you hear from him. I'll call you if I find out anything or if he shows up here. Take care and try not to worry. "

Crystal hung up and dialed the police station.

"Town Police," a female voice chirped on the other end of the phone.

"Michael Blackburn, please," Crystal said, trying to sound calm and professional.

"Michael Blackburn, Missing Persons."

"Michael, this is Crystal," she said frantically, starting to blurt out everything Gloria had told her.

"Slow down, Crystal. I can barely understand a word you're saying," Michael interrupted. "Don't panic. I'll see what I can find out and call you back."

Not long after Crystal hung up the telephone, there was a knock on the door. Michael stood there with a somber look on his face.

"Crystal, we need to talk. Can I come in?"

"Sure, sit down. What's wrong? Is it Uncle Frank?"

As she sat next to him on the chesterfield, Michael took her hand.

"Frank's been arrested and is in a holding cell at the police station. I picked him up at the mill yesterday. I wanted to make sure of everything before telling you.

When you moved in and told me about growing up with Frank and moving around the country, I thought it sounded strange. I did some checking, and it turns out Frank is not your uncle. He was a neighbour of yours in Calgary, where you're from. You were kidnapped at the age of four by Samuel Boutilier. Your parents have been searching for you ever since."

Crystal could hardly believe what he was saying. What was he talking about? Did he say she had been kidnapped? Crystal looked at him in disbelief. She started to say something, and Michael interrupted her.

"Wait until I'm finished the whole story – there's more. I knew your name and birthday, so I started going back over the national missing persons list. Your parents have never given up looking for you. Whenever the police got close to catching Samuel, he would pack up and move before they could arrest him.

The Calgary police force has kept updating the file, with the hopes that they might catch him and find you. He had a wife and little girl who died in a fire. His little girl was about your age when he kidnapped you. I didn't say anything to you because I wanted to be sure. Yesterday I was positive, so I arrested Frank, or Samuel Boutilier, and after a long interrogation, he finally confessed."

Crystal sat astonished, barely breathing, trying to digest what Michael was telling her.

"My parents are alive?" she asked slowly.

"Yes, they are. They'll be here today. They flew into Deer Lake from Calgary late last night. We need them to identify Samuel," Michael told her cautiously, waiting for a reaction to let him know how Crystal was taking the news.

"All this time, I thought you might be interested in me. How could I have been so naïve? All you were doing was an investigation?" Crystal's tears started to flow uncontrollably down her cheeks and onto her lap.

Crystal sat void of all feeling. Michael had been doing an investigation. He had not been falling in love with her. That was a hard enough pill to swallow, but now she would have to come face to face with her mother and father, whom she thought were dead. What would they think of her? What would she think of them? She tried to imagine their faces in her mind but couldn't remember. Would she recognize them? Then there was Uncle Frank, or Samuel. He had kidnapped her. How could he have done such a thing? He had lied to her for years. Michael had lied, too. Her whole life had been a lie.

The doorbell rang, interrupting their conversation, and Michael got up to answer it. A man and woman entered the living room. "Thank God you're safe," the woman said, moving swiftly towards her. "We never gave up believing you were still alive and would be found."

She was an older version of who Crystal saw in the mirror every morning. She had the same dark eyes that showed the struggle she was dealing with, even though her face was lacking any kind of emotion. The dress she wore was navy blue and fit her perfectly. It showed definite style and looked like an original design. Her shoes matched the colour of her dress and were obviously hand sewn and made of expensive leather.

She took Michael's place on the chesterfield beside Crystal. "We owe finding you to Michael. His instincts told him something was wrong. We're so relieved you're safe and will finally be coming home."

Crystal looked across the room at the tall man standing near the door. He was well over six feet tall, with a slender build. He was middle-aged with silver-gray hair that had been recently cut. He wore a black blazer over a plain white t-shirt and loose-fitting blue jeans. He hadn't spoken a word. He stood staring at her with tears streaming down his cheeks.

"I don't know what I'm going to do. Everything's happening so fast," Crystal said, hesitantly.

"You can't consider staying here. Where will you live? What will you do? Things are different now. You have a home and a family who love you. You must come home with us. We have so much to catch up on," the woman said, looking at the man standing by the door as if trying to will him to say something.

"Jonathan, make her realize she must come home," the woman said.

"She's a grown woman, Amanda," he said in a voice that was soft and low.

Crystal was so confused; she didn't know what to do. This woman was asking her to go home. She didn't have a home. How could she go back after all that had happened? She couldn't face people she didn't know. She wanted to stay with Michael and Katie. She loved them. She didn't have anywhere to go, any place where she felt like she belonged.

The only man she thought she belonged with, Uncle Frank, had turned out to be a fraud. He was sitting in a jail cell downtown. She needed time to think and figure out what she was going to do. Where was she going to go? She turned and looked at Michael, silently begging for him to rescue her.

"She could live with Katie and me. Katie needs a

babysitter and loves spending time with Crystal. She'll have to testify in court anyway, and that would keep her from having to fly back here," Michael suggested.

"I don't think that's a good idea. Crystal has a family of her own. I think she should come home with us. When she has to testify, we'll come back," Amanda said sharply.

Crystal shot a surprised glance at Michael, grateful for his sudden offer. Here was a way for her to take her time in deciding where she wanted to go and what she was going to do.

"We'll have lots of time to catch up. I'm twenty-three – I'm not a kid anymore – and I want to stay with Michael and Katie. Please understand that I need time to figure out how I feel about things," Crystal said.

"I don't understand, dear, but I'll try. It's hard to believe you're a grown woman. I've missed so much of your life," Amanda said, her voice filled with emotion.

Michael took Jonathan outside, and Crystal took Amanda into the kitchen. "I'll make coffee and we can talk. You can tell me everything I should know about myself and don't," Crystal suggested, trying to sound cheerful.

"Crystal, did Samuel hurt you in anyway?" Amanda whispered.

Crystal stopped and looked at her.

"Amanda, if you're asking me whether he beat or abused me in any way, the answer is no."

"Well, dear, you hear so many horror stories in the news about children who've been abducted and treated poorly."

Crystal began to shake with anger. "Samuel was an alcoholic, and we moved a lot, but he never once touched me in a way that would be considered mean, abusive, or inappropriate. He tried to make my life happy in every way he could, no matter what the circumstances. I think, after a while, he genuinely believed I was his dead daughter. I'm not saying what he did was right – I'm just trying to understand why he did it, and what made him think he had the right to disrupt the life of a little girl."

Michael and Crystal sat in the yard after Amanda and Jonathan had returned to their hotel. The moon glowed, and the stars overhead flickered like a million tiny candles.

"Thank you for agreeing to be Katie's nanny," he said quietly.

"I did it for Katie. I'm not certain how long I'll stay. I'll probably go to Calgary and try to put the pieces of my life back together."

"Oh, Crystal, I do like you. In fact, I've fallen in love with you. I suggested you stay on as Katie's babysitter because I can't bear the thought of you leaving and moving someplace else. I would like to get this case out of the way so we can start fresh. What do you say? Can we do that?" he asked, sounding hopeful.

"That would be wonderful. I've loved you and Katie almost from the first moment we met."

"I'd like to move slow, more for my own sake than for Katie's," Michael continued, moving closer to her. "If she had her way, you and I would be waltzing up the aisle tomorrow."

"That's quite all right. I'd like to take it slow, too. There's been so much to absorb about myself. This is my very first meaningful relationship. I want to enjoy the romance."

Crystal replied shyly.

Michael stood up, preparing to leave. Crystal stood up beside him, and they gazed into each other's eyes. "I'd better get home. Good night, Crystal," Michael whispered, and turned to walk away.

"Good night, Michael," Crystal cooed, and she stepped over the threshold and closed the door behind her.

The next morning, Crystal woke up exhausted. The events of the previous day had played over and over in her mind and kept her tossing and turning all night. Could it all have been a bad dream? She got up and padded to the kitchen to start the coffee brewing while she took a shower. The familiar face in the mirror looked different somehow. She kept hoping to hear her Uncle Frank's gruff voice yelling at her through the door to hurry up.

She stepped out of the shower and opened the bathroom door. The aroma of coffee perking in the kitchen floated down the hallway as a blast of frigid air hit her. She went to the bedroom and pulled on a pair of jeans and a sweater. She brushed her hair, tied her Nikes, and went back to the kitchen.

As she sat drinking her coffee and nibbling on a piece of toast, she decided the only way to find out what was going on was to go to the station to see Samuel and talk to him directly. She would have to get used to calling him Samuel, since to her he would always be Uncle Frank.

She picked up the phone and dialed the police station number.

"Town Police," a female voice answered at the other end.

"Hello, I was wondering when visiting hours are for

prisoners? I'd like to make arrangements to see one," Crystal said.

"Usually there's no problem during the day to visit a prisoner. The best thing to do is drop in. Who is it you'd like to see? I can tell you if there are any restrictions surrounding visitation for that prisoner."

"I'd like to see Samuel Boutilier," Crystal said, trying to keep her voice from quivering.

"Mr. Boutilier is here. All visitors must make arrangements to see him through Constable Blackburn, the arresting officer. Would you like me to transfer your call?"

"Yes, please and thank you."

"Michael Blackburn, Missing Persons."

"Michael, it's Crystal. I want to see Samuel. The receptionist said I had to make arrangements through you. Can I come down and see him?" Her voice was barely audible.

"Crystal, I don't think that's a good idea. I was afraid you would try to see him. That's why I had all visitor requests transferred to me. He's had people in who work with him, and Gloria's been here. I think it would be best if you didn't see him. You'll be testifying against him in court. I don't know how he'd react to you now."

"Michael, I'd really like to talk to him, please. He's the only family I've ever known. I'd like to make sure he's all right," she pleaded.

"Crystal, you must remember that he kidnapped you. He took you away from your family and transported you all over the country for his own selfish reasons. I don't want you forgetting that."

"I know he did, Michael. Believe me, no one has thought

about what he did more than I have. I still need to talk to him. Please let me see him, just once. I have to find out what was going on in his head and why he did what he did."

"All right, Crystal. Once, no more. And only if I'm with you."

"No, Michael, it must be alone. He's not going to talk to me with you standing around. It must be alone."

"I don't like it, Crystal, and the visit won't be long," he said after a long pause.

"I'll make it as quick as possible, I promise. And thank you," Crystal said, hanging up the telephone.

She finished her coffee and pulled her denim jacket from the closet. Her mind started to spin with questions she needed answered. She went outside and hopped into the front seat of the old Toyota and turned out onto the street. Ten minutes later, she pulled into the parking lot of the police station. She walked up the front steps and nodded at two police officers coming toward her. Her legs wobbled slightly with nervousness as she pushed open the huge glass doors and walked inside. The girl behind the plexiglass window peered through and asked, "Can I help you?"

"I'd like to see Michael Blackburn," Crystal stammered.

"Have a seat. I'll get him," she replied and disappeared.

Michael appeared, and when she looked at him, her heart began to pound uncontrollably as he moved towards the door.

"Are you sure you want to do this?" he asked as he opened the door for her to walk through.

"Yes, I am. I have to. Thank you for letting me come," Crystal said, stepping through the open door to follow

Michael down the hallway.

Crystal followed him into the depths of the police station. The sound of telephones and police officers talking drifted into the background. A couple of the police officers glanced at Crystal as she walked behind Michael and he ushered her through an open door into the interrogation room.

"You wait in here. I'll get him," Michael said, closing the door behind him.

The room was bare except for a wooden table and two wooden chairs. Crystal sat down and looked around. There was a smoked glass window along one wall and two fluorescent lights in the ceiling covered with wire. The walls were painted a hideous pale green that was almost gray.

The door opened and Crystal turned. Samuel entered with Michael behind him. Crystal stood up and walked towards them.

"Hello, Samuel," she said in a whisper.

Samuel stared at her. She had never seen him look so old. He looked like he had aged twenty years in two days. The orange coveralls he wore were two sizes too big, and there were no laces in his sneakers. His eyes were dull and lifeless. He was unshaven, with beard stubble covering the lower half of his jaw. His hands shook, and he grabbed at them to make them stop. The lack of alcohol during his time in jail was starting to reveal the extent of his alcoholism.

"Michael, can you please leave us alone?" Crystal asked, motioning Samuel to one of the chairs.

"Crystal, what are you doing here? You're the last person I expected to see after all that's happened," he said in a feeble voice.

"I wanted to talk to you. I need to hear your side of the story," Crystal muttered.

They sat down, and she looked across the table at him. His hands were shaking, and tears started to well up in his eyes. He swiped them away with the back of his hand.

"I'm sorry for everything, Crystal. I hoped you'd never find out the truth. I know now that was impossible. They wouldn't leave us alone. Everything would've been fine if they'd just left us alone," he said, his voice trembling as he spoke.

"Samuel, tell me everything from the beginning. Why did you do it? What were you thinking?"

Samuel leaned his elbows on the table and put his hands over his face, rubbing his eyes.

"It all started with the fire. I don't know what I was thinking. I loved them so much. It seemed so unfair. They were both so young. Penelope was only four. She didn't deserve to die, and her mother was so beautiful. We were an incredibly happy family. I couldn't understand why it was them and not me. I was working when it happened. The fireman said there was nothing they could do. The house went up so fast. They were asleep in bed and that was it. Gone, both of them.

I moved into the house next door to your parents once it was over. You looked so much like Penelope. I watched you play and laugh in the backyard. I would talk to you over the fence, and you would look up at me with your big dark eyes and smile. I honestly believed at the time that it was the right thing for me to do.

One day when your father was away on business, your

25

brother Allen fell and broke his arm. Your mother asked me to babysit you while she rushed Allen to the hospital. I did, and before I knew it, we were on our way east. I told you about the car accident and that I was your Uncle Frank. You cried at first, but in a couple of days you were happy. I took you to every attraction we passed on the road. I didn't know where I was going. I just kept driving. We drove for about a week and stopped in a small town outside of Winnipeg. I got a job working for a contracting outfit as a labourer.

The police bulletins and Amber Alerts came out. Someone would recognize me with you, and we would have to move. The rest is the same. Every time the police would get close, or someone would get suspicious and start asking questions, we would move on. As you got older, your looks started to change, and we didn't have to move so much. It took people longer to put two and two together, but the police kept coming."

"How could you do it? How could you live with yourself knowing you had taken someone else's child?" Crystal asked. "I wasn't yours to take."

"I don't know. I guess that's why I drank so much. After a while, I was used to you being around. I loved having you with me. It was just you and me. To me, you were my little girl. I couldn't take you back or turn myself in. If I did, I would lose you, too. I loved you like my own. I was never mean to you was I, Crystal? I didn't treat you badly, did I?"

"No, Samuel, you didn't. That still doesn't make it right. You took me from my family. You lied to me all this time. You say you love me, but if you really loved me, how could you take everything away from me?" She began to cry, and her lower lip quivered.

"I wanted to have my own little girl. I wanted to watch you grow up, look after you, make sure you were happy. Watch you fall in love for the first time and walk you down the aisle. Do the things with you that I would've done with my Penelope. Be your father."

"Samuel, you were my father, but you robbed me of what was rightfully mine," she said, reaching out and touching his arm.

Even after all she knew, she couldn't get angry at him as she looked across the table. He loved her. She could see it in his eyes; she was his daughter. He had witnessed all her successes and failures. He had comforted her when she was upset and nursed her when she was sick. He had protected her from all the monsters when she was little, told her about boys and encouraged her when she was depressed. No matter what her biological connection was to the people she had met the night before, Samuel had been her father, and she couldn't stand to see him like this.

She had talked to Gloria briefly the night before, and Gloria loved him more than any other woman he had ever been involved with. She was incredibly upset over the circumstances. She said that she would stand by him.

Crystal sat in the interrogation room of the police station trying to unscramble his actions for the past twenty years. She couldn't be the one to bring it all tumbling down on him. He had been there for her, and although it wasn't right, it was all she knew. She stood up and walked towards the door.

Samuel looked at her and said, "Crystal, I'm sorry. I'm so

sorry for everything."

Crystal nodded as she opened the door.

"Michael, I'm ready to go."

Samuel got up and walked towards Michael, his feet scuffing the floor. "Take me back," he said, his voice barely audible.

Michael looked at Crystal and pointed towards a door. "You can sit in my office. I'll be right back."

Crystal watched him lead Samuel through a heavy steel door and listened to the hollow echo as it slammed behind them. She went into Michael's office, sank into one of the two armchairs, and looked around. Michael's desk was piled with paperwork and files. There was a picture of his late wife and Katie on one corner next to a telephone.

The chair she was sitting in was midnight blue, and the carpet on the floor was the same colour as the chair. There was a coffee pot on a buffet table to the far side of the wall, surrounded by sugar, coffee creamer, cups, and stir sticks. She got up and helped herself to the coffee. There were books piled everywhere, filing cabinets lined the far wall, and a rubber tree sat in the corner behind the door.

Michael was right. She should not have come to see Samuel. Now she couldn't testify against him. She wanted this over and wanted to get on with her life.

Michael entered the office and walked straight to the coffee pot. He poured himself a cup and then dropped into the high-back, black leather chair that sat behind his desk. He took a mouthful of coffee and sat looking at her.

"Michael, I can't do it," Crystal said.

"Listen, that man is not your Uncle Frank! He's a man

who kidnapped you. He took you from your parents and dragged you all over this country to keep you from them. Crystal, he's a criminal and deserves to pay for what he's taken from you, for what he's done to your life."

"I've thought about it. In fact, I thought about it all last night – I couldn't think of anything else. That's why I had to see him today, talk to him, look into his eyes, and try to figure out what made the man tick. Do you know it's the first time I've tried to do that? When I was growing up, he was there for me.

I know he's not my Uncle Frank, but that still does not change the past twenty years. He's looked after me, comforted me, and encouraged me. He was good to me. He did everything any biological parent would've done. He gave me all he could. I can't testify against him in court. I can't be the one to put him away."

"Crystal, if you don't testify willingly, I may have you called as a hostile witness," Michael said slowly, letting the sentence hang in the air.

"You mean you can make me testify, even if I don't want to?" Crystal asked, surprised.

"Yes, it'll be harder for the Crown Prosecutor to accept a hostile witness, but we can force you to testify. You'll have to tell the truth once you're on the witness stand."

"Michael, I can't do that! I can't be the one to send him to jail. Please don't force me to testify against him. I can't sit up there, look at him, and testify to what he's done. Why won't they let him go? Gloria loves him, and they would be happy together. He knows what he did was wrong, and you know he'll never do it again. He's been living with this nightmare for twenty years. It's over. Why can't you let him go? I want to forget this ever happened."

Crystal was tired of the whole ordeal. She wanted to go back to being Crystal, Uncle Frank's niece who didn't have a mother or father. She wanted to go back to being Katie's babysitter and waiting for Michael to come home from work. She wanted to sit in his living room the way they had last week.

"Your mother and father won't like it. They feel they've been robbed of your childhood. This man took their child. They want him to pay for what he's done. They're not going to stand by and let him walk away," he said, sitting up and leaning towards her across the desk.

"I'll talk to my mother and father, make them understand I can't go through with it. If I can get them to drop the charges, will you see if the Crown Prosecutor will do the same?"

Michael sat silent for a long time. Crystal could see by the look on his face that he was not happy.

"Please, Michael," she begged him. "If you've ever felt anything for me, don't make me go through with this. I'll talk to my mother and father, and you talk to the Crown Prosecutor. I know if you tell him you don't have enough evidence to proceed, he'll listen to you. They're not going to want to get into the courtroom and have problems. They'll want to have an open-and-shut case. I'm not going to hurt Samuel on purpose.

Maybe if he had to live here and was released into Gloria's custody, continue to work at the mill, get counselling. You'd be here – you could keep an eye on him. There must be a way you can get the Crown to agree. Please try."

Michael still hadn't said a word. Crystal could see him studying her face, looking for something. He was struggling with her decision. She knew it wouldn't be easy for him. She also knew she couldn't testify against Samuel, and she was going to do everything in her power to help him stay out of jail. Crystal knew Michael could see that; he could see she was determined to get the matter dropped before it went any further.

"Look, Crystal, I can understand what you're saying, and I can understand why, believe me. Are you sure, though? I don't want you to regret this decision down the road. I don't know how your parents are going to handle this. They may want to proceed regardless," he said, draining the last drop of coffee from his cup.

"I'll make them understand. Really, I will. Please do this for me, Michael," she said meeting him halfway across the desk and laying her hand on top of his.

"Let me get on with my life. I want to put this behind me, pick up the pieces and start over. I'll talk to Amanda and Jonathan and talk to Gloria. I'll see if she would be willing to be responsible for Samuel. He could live with her on house arrest or something. You could set the conditions."

Michael took her hand and looked straight at her. "All right, all right. I'll see what I can do. I'm not going to promise you anything. The Crown Prosecutor may want to go ahead with this one. This isn't a minor offense. I'll tell him everything you've told me and see what he says. That's the best I can do."

"Oh, Michael, I love you! I love you so much. Thank

you!" She stood up and leaned across the desk, throwing her arms around his neck.

He stood up and walked towards the door. The police officers sitting at their desks were staring at them through the glass window of his office door.

"You'd better go. The guys will wonder what's going on. I'll see you at home tonight. You talk to your parents and Gloria. I'll talk to the Crown Prosecutor. Don't get your hopes up. I may not be able to do anything."

He opened the door, and she walked through. The police officers watched closely as they walked by. "Where's Katie this morning?" Michael asked, sounding more like himself.

"I left her with Gloria so I could come down here. She's really confused about what's going on. I'll try to explain it to her. Thank you again, Michael, for everything," she said, making her way out the glass doors that led to the street.

Chapter 3

GLORIA OPENED THE FRONT DOOR before Crystal could get out of the car.

"Did you see him? How is he?" she asked anxiously.

"Yes, I saw him, and he's fine. Where's Katie?" Crystal asked, looking around.

"She's behind the house playing with Jeremy from next door. She's fine. Come in – we'll have coffee on the deck. We can watch them and talk at the same time."

Gloria's place was like a dollhouse. The kitchen was decorated in white with the cupboards trimmed in red. There were wicker baskets and plants hanging everywhere. Large patio doors led from the dining room onto a deck and into the backyard. Crystal stood in the doorway watching Katie and Jeremy play in a sandbox beneath a towering pine tree in the back of the yard. Katie turned and waved.

Gloria poured coffee, and they took the steaming mugs

outside. Crystal took a mouthful and turned to Gloria. Her green eyes shone like emeralds as she talked. Her fiery red hair fell in ringlets and bounced as she walked. Her small, delicate nose was speckled with freckles, and her cream-coloured skin showed no sign of her forty years.

"I didn't want to say anything before I talked to Samuel. I wasn't sure what I was going to do or how I would feel. I've decided to try to help him," Crystal said slowly.

"What do you mean?" Gloria asked cautiously.

"I've refused to testify against Samuel. Michael said I could be called as a hostile witness, but he would talk to the Crown Prosecutor. I'm going to try to convince my parents not to go through with prosecuting him. I want to put this behind me. I'm hoping they'll agree with me and leave it at that."

"Do you think they'll go for it?" Gloria asked, taking a mouthful of coffee. "I'd love to see him set free. I don't think he was thinking straight the day he kidnapped you. Crystal, I love Samuel and hate the thought of him spending any time in jail. If he must, I'll wait for him."

"I agree with you, Gloria. Samuel is a good man at heart. I think we should both be able to start fresh. Michael and I have talked about the conditions he'll suggest to the Crown. I wanted to run them by you since you'd be involved."

"What kind of conditions, Crystal?" she asked thoughtfully.

"One condition would be that Samuel would be under house arrest and live here with you. He would be unable to move away and would have to lead a stable lifestyle. He would seek counseling and continue working at the mill.

Michael would be able to keep an eye on him and know what he's doing," Crystal explained, closely studying Gloria's reaction.

Gloria's eyes lit up. "That would do it? I'd agree to have Samuel live here under house arrest and keep an eye on him. I love him. I've lived in this town all my life and couldn't move or live anywhere else. If Samuel would agree and could keep his job at the mill, we'd be fine living here together. Michael could come over anytime he wanted to see Samuel."

"Are you sure you wouldn't mind?" Crystal questioned her again.

"Look, Crystal, from the first time Samuel walked into the diner and we met, we hit it off. The more time we spent together, the more I knew he was the man for me. I know he didn't tell me the complete truth, but he's a good man and I love him."

"Michael couldn't promise anything. I still have to talk to my parents. I'm going to see what I can do. If you agree and Samuel agrees, we should be able to work something out."

"You'll get nothing but cooperation from me," Gloria said, smiling.

Crystal stood up. "I have to meet my parents. I'd like to talk this over with them."

Crystal turned to Gloria. "I'll do what I can. Try not to worry."

"I know you will, Crystal. I hope it'll all be over soon for you and Samuel."

As Crystal drove into town, her mind began to whirl with thoughts of how to explain things to her parents. She didn't know how she was going to convince them that letting Samuel go free was the only way to put the past behind her.

Crystal parked the car and entered the restaurant attached to the hotel where her parents were staying. It was a tiny place, and she easily spotted her parents sitting in a booth. They looked so out of place. Amanda was dressed in the same designer dress from the day before. Her dark, graying hair was pulled back in a tight French roll, and her large diamond stud earrings sparkled as the rays from the sun through the window danced off them. Jonathan was dressed in a gray suit. Crystal smiled at Nora, the waitress, and asked for a glass of water before sliding into the seat across from them.

"Hi. I'm sorry I'm late," she said nervously.

"We weren't sure you'd come at all, dear. Last night was such a shock to all of us. We've been searching for you for so long it's hard to believe you're sitting across from us. I don't see how you can consider staying in this place. You must come back to Calgary with us." Amanda stated matter-of-factly.

"Amanda, we must give her a chance to get used to the idea of having us as parents before she can make that kind of decision. She must be very unsure of how she feels," Jonathan said quietly.

Jonathan was soft-spoken and had a gentle manner rarely found in a person. His brown eyes held compassion and seemed to understand that she had something important she wanted to discuss with them.

"I went to see Samuel at the police station this morning," Crystal announced in a voice that cracked when she tried to speak.

"Oh, Crystal," Amanda said quickly. "Do you think that was such a good idea? That man is a terrible criminal. I don't think you should be around him any longer. Look at what he did to us. I still can't believe it took twenty years to find you. That goes to show you what kind of a man he truly is. He was smart enough to move you as soon as the police got close to arresting him. I'm so happy Constable Blackburn acted immediately, or he may have gotten away again."

"Amanda, please listen to me and try to understand how I feel about all of this. I've thought long and hard about my decision and have talked to Samuel and Michael about it. I've discussed it with Gloria, Samuel's girlfriend. We're all in agreement. You must listen and try to understand what I've decided to do," Crystal said firmly.

"Crystal, this doesn't sound good," Amanda said, a note of fear creeping into her voice.

"Amanda, let the girl talk," Jonathan interrupted, turning towards Amanda. "We must remember, she's a grown woman with a mind of her own. She's certainly old enough to know what she wants and to make her own decisions."

"All right, I'll listen to what you have to say," Amanda said, looking down like a scolded child.

"I went to see Samuel this morning. I wanted to hear his side of the story. After talking with him, I spoke to Michael about not wanting to testify against him in court."

Amanda let out a heavy sigh but remained silent. Jonathan said nothing; he sat and watched her carefully as she spoke.

"Michael didn't agree with me and threatened to have me called as a hostile witness. I begged him not to and presented him with an option, which is that Samuel goes free with the following conditions."

Crystal reviewed the conditions regarding Gloria and the Crown Prosecutor. Crystal could see Jonathan's eyes were full of understanding and sympathy. He knew what she was saying, and it was obvious he was in full agreement with her. Amanda was not so understanding. Her eyes grew cold and calculating. She made Crystal nervous, and Crystal listened intently as Amanda spoke sternly. "What are you going to do? Are you planning to stay here, or are you planning to return to Calgary with us?"

"I'm planning to stay here, look after Katie, and explore my relationship with Michael." Crystal replied.

"I still don't think that's a good idea. We can offer you so many opportunities. We'd like to get to know you. You're our daughter in case you've forgotten. We love you, which is why we have spent the last twenty years of our lives looking for you. No, I think you should return with us to Alberta." Amanda said solemnly.

"Amanda, let her go. She's not ours anymore," Jonathan said, as tears began to well up in his eyes.

"No, Jonathan – I won't have it! We've lived through hell every day, hoping there would be word they had found her alive. The least she can do is come home with us and give us a chance. She's willing to let that despicable man get off scot-free. I will not let it go!" Amanda retorted.

Amanda turned to Crystal, her eyes filled with anger. As she gathered her composure, her voice was ice cold. "If you can let Samuel get away with what he has done, then you must come home with us. He won't be in jail, so you'll be able to see him. Nothing will have changed for you. But for us, we've searched for you for twenty years. Then we come here, and you decide to stay, living in the same town with that man. No! I will not have it! If you want us to drop the charges, then you'll have to come home. That's the only way I will agree to this," she demanded.

Crystal couldn't believe what she was hearing. This woman was asking her to give up everything important to her, to give up Michael and Katie. "I can't go back with you. There's Michael and Katie. I love them. I don't want to go back with you. Please don't make me choose between them, Samuel, and you." Crystal's voice was barely a whisper.

"No, Crystal! If you want Samuel to stay out of jail, you must return to Calgary," Amanda shot back. "One year should be enough time to see if you like living at home."

"Amanda, let her go. She's happy here. If she comes home with us, she'll be miserable. She's not a little girl anymore," Jonathan said, trying to hide his disappointment.

Amanda turned towards Jonathan in the booth, her words seeping from her thin lips like venom. "I gave birth to this girl, loved her, and fed her for the first four years of her life. I'm her natural mother. Because of that bastard Samuel Boutilier, I've missed the last twenty years. I'm asking for one year. If she thinks she's in love with this Michael Blackburn and if he's truly in love with her, then their love will last for one year. It's not much to ask for the pain and agony we've suffered in trying to find her."

She turned to Crystal once again and said, "If you want Samuel free, then you'll come home with us for one year. That's the only way I'll agree."

"Amanda, please! Don't ask me to do this. I can't leave Michael and Katie." Crystal began to cry openly, her tears splashing in the remnants of the water in her glass. Her stomach felt like she had swallowed a lead ball, and she thought she was going to be sick. What would she tell Michael? How could she tell Katie?

This woman who Crystal thought would be compassionate, loving, and understanding was hard and cruel. Amanda didn't care about her. She only cared about herself and what she wanted. She was an unfeeling, merciless woman with a heart of stone.

Crystal looked around and located the clock hanging on the wall. She then stood up, looking down at them. "Two o'clock, I must go. Katie will be wondering where I am."

Amanda looked up. "We're leaving Friday. I'll make the arrangements for you to travel with us. If you decide to stay, I will push this to the full extent of the law. Do you understand?"

"Yes, I understand fully," Crystal replied, walking out the door and feeling relieved to be away from her.

Crystal sat behind the wheel for a long time before starting the car. What was she going to do? How could Amanda ask her to leave? Her friends and her life were here. A year seemed like an eternity. At least Samuel would be free to have a life and start over with Gloria. She started the car and thought, Michael, what will I ever do without you?

"You're going to do what?" Michael exclaimed when she told him. "Crystal, you can't leave! I love you! What about Katie? What about all the things we've said? I don't want you to leave!"

Crystal watched him pace back and forth between the kitchen and the living room. She could see this was tearing him apart.

"I don't have a choice, Michael. Amanda is determined. The only way she'll give up is if I return to Calgary for a year. It's only a year, Michael. I love you and Katie, but the only way we can put this behind us is to get these people out of my life. She doesn't care about anyone other than herself. She wants her little girl under her roof no matter what. I can't stay. I must close this chapter of my life. I couldn't become involved with you knowing Samuel is sitting in a jail cell for the rest of his life and we're the ones who put him there."

Michael walked towards the bar and poured himself a shot of whiskey. "You want something?" he asked, motioning towards the liquor lined up against the wall at the back of the bar.

"A glass of red wine, thank you. Michael, we can get through this – I know we can. When I come back, we'll start over. I love you, and my feelings are not going to change. We can talk on the phone, email, and text. You and Katie could come to Calgary for a visit. We could take her to the Calgary Stampede. I bet she would love that." Crystal tried to sound cheerful.

"Marry me, Crystal. We'll get married before you leave. Then, you go to Calgary for a year and come back," Michael said, passing her a glass of wine.

Crystal smiled up at him. "Michael, I can't do that. What if your feelings change in a year?"

Crystal knew he was grasping at straws. She wanted to

marry him and spend the rest of her life with him, but she couldn't agree, not under the circumstances. She had to walk away and pray that she could walk back into his life once the year was over, and things would remain as they were now.

"Do you want me to talk to Katie?" Crystal asked, breaking the silence.

"No, I'll tell her. She's not going to understand why you're going. I'll try to make it as easy as possible for her. I can't believe you're doing this for Samuel. He ruined your life."

"Samuel isn't the one ruining my life. It's Amanda. She's the one forcing me to go to Calgary. I don't know why she would want me in Calgary, knowing I'll resent her for tearing me away from you and Katie."

"Tomorrow's Thursday. Can we spend the day together? I'll take the day off, and we can go to the beach for the day. I'll call Gloria and see if she can look after Katie. I have to go to the station in the morning, I want to talk to Samuel. I'll be free at about ten."

"I'd like that. Don't worry Michael – we'll get through this. I know you're the only man for me, and I'll be back in a year. I promise," Crystal said, placing her hand on his arm.

Michael shifted position to face her and put his glass on the coffee table. He took her into his arms and kissed her passionately on the lips. "I love you, Crystal. I love you so much," he whispered against her cheek.

Crystal ran her fingers through his hair, feeling the silkiness of the black waves against her hand. "I love you too, Michael. That's why I must do this. Please try to understand."

"Stay with me tonight, Crystal. I want to make love to you."

"No, Michael, not like this," she whispered, as she set down the wine glass in preparation to leave.

Her heart was breaking as she walked towards the door, leaving Michael sitting on the chesterfield while he watched her leave.

Chapter 4

MICHAEL STOPPED TO PICK UP Crystal after dropping Katie at Gloria's and driving to the station. "Did you speak to Samuel? Did he agree to the terms?" Crystal asked, pouring him a cup of coffee.

"Yes, of course he did. He was surprised you'd go to all this trouble to keep him out of prison. He's more than willing to cooperate. I've planned for him to receive professional counselling and I spoke to Gloria when I dropped Katie off.

Your parents stopped by the office and dropped the charges. Believe me, the Crown Prosecutor isn't thrilled. He wanted me to try to persuade you to reconsider. I told him there was no changing your mind. Can we forget all this and just enjoy each other's company on your last day here?"

"Yes, Michael. I want to forget all about it for today," Crystal said, kissing him delicately on the cheek.

The sun was warm, and they had the beach completely to themselves. They talked, drank wine, and feasted on cheese, crackers, and grapes. They walked along the beach, laughed, cried, and laid on a blanket staring up at the clouds. When the sun began to sink slowly towards the horizon, Michael rolled towards her on the blanket and took her in his arms. Crystal curled into his side and laid her head on his chest. They stayed that way in silence watching the sunset over the water. Crystal didn't know how she was going to leave him, and she hoped that when it was over, he'd love her as much as she loved him.

The next morning, rain was falling, and Crystal could hear it lightly tapping against her bedroom window. She stretched and laid in bed staring at the ceiling. Yesterday had been the most wonderful day. She rolled over and glanced at the clock. Michael was picking her up in an hour to take her to the airport. It had been almost unbearable to say goodbye to Katie the night before. Crystal tried to explain to her that it was only for a year, and she'd be back.

Crystal was finishing getting dressed when the door-bell rang.

"Hi, Michael," she said, wearily opening the door.

"Hi, Crystal. Are you sure you want to do this? It's not too late to change your mind."

"I know. I would love to stay, but I have to go. The time will go fast. How's Katie?"

"She's not sure what's going on. She's trying to understand."

"I'm going to miss you both. Maybe you driving me to the airport wasn't such a great idea," Crystal said, as tears began to spill over her cheeks.

Michael picked up her bags and packed them into the trunk of his car. Crystal took one last look at the house where her past, present, and future had fused. She was going to miss it here.

Crystal slid in the front seat next to him and turned on the radio as a distraction. The songs did nothing to improve her mood. They both sat silent, engrossed in their own thoughts of what the future would hold for them. They parked the car at the airport, and Michael helped Crystal take her luggage to the check-in counter.

"The plane doesn't leave for a couple of hours. Do you want to get a cup of coffee?" Crystal asked, as she walked back to where he was waiting for her.

"Coffee sounds great," he said, taking her hand.

Crystal looked through the coffee shop window and watched the people walk by. "Don't worry, Michael. We'll keep in touch, and before you know it, I'll be back and this will seem like a bad dream."

"I wish I'd never decided to try to figure out who you were. That way, none of this would've happened. You wouldn't be going anywhere. You'd be staying here with Katie and me."

"There's no use dwelling on what's already taken place. We have to concentrate on getting through this mess so we can be together."

Crystal looked up and sighed. Amanda and Jonathan were standing in the doorway. Amanda smiled when she spotted them and started to move across the room.

"There you are. We thought you might be running late.

I called your brother Allen. He's going to meet us at the airport. He's so excited we've found you," Amanda said, sitting down next to Michael.

"I don't remember having a brother. It'll be good to meet him, but when my year is up in Calgary, I'll return here to be with Michael and Katie."

"We'll see," Amanda interrupted. "I'm sure once you find out who you are, it won't take you long to settle down with us."

Crystal looked at Michael apologetically as the loud-speaker sounded that it was time to board the flight. They all stood up slowly. Michael put his arm around Crystal and said, "I'll walk you to security. Are you sure I can't make you change your mind?"

While they said goodbye at the gate, Amanda and Jonathan were like sentinels watching their every move and word. Michael took her in his arms and pulled her close. She breathed in the spicy smell of his cologne and put her arms around him to draw him closer.

"Crystal, come on! There's no need for this. It's time to board," Amanda said sharply, taking her arm.

Crystal drew Michael closer and whispered, "I love you, Michael. I'll be back."

"I love you, too, Crystal. No matter what, Katie and I will be waiting for you. Come home soon," he said, his voice filled with emotion.

"That's enough, you two. She'll be fine with us, Michael. You don't have to worry about her. Thank you for all your help. We're truly grateful for all you've done," Amanda said, grabbing Crystal by the arm and steering her away.

Amanda nudged Crystal ahead of her to move her through security. Crystal took one last look at Michael, who stood waving, before she turned and walked away through the crowd.

"Don't worry, sweetheart. Once you get to Calgary, your father and I will introduce you to a lot of nice young men that work at our computer company. It won't take you long to forget this little one-horse town and everyone in it."

They boarded the plane, and it wasn't long before they were soaring west through the clouds. *What am I doing?* Crystal thought. Confusion seemed to be her best friend. She tried to look on the bright side. It was exciting to think that she would soon meet a brother she never knew existed.

She sat next to Amanda and listened to her ramble on about the computer company they owned and how wonderful Calgary was going to be. She tried to imagine what her future was going to look like, and what awaited her in Alberta. The best way to get through this horrible separation from Michael was to keep busy and not wallow in depression. She closed her eyes and leaned her head against the window. She heard the flight attendant ask if there was anything she could get her. Crystal shook her head. All she wanted was to be left alone until the plane descended onto the runway in her new home city.

"Crystal! Crystal, wake up, dear. We're here. We're home!" Amanda said excitedly, taking her arm gently and giving her a little shake.

Crystal rubbed the sleep out of her eyes and glanced out the window of the plane. She stood up and followed Amanda and Jonathan. "Welcome to Calgary. Thank you for flying with us. I hope you enjoyed your flight," the flight attendant said sweetly, as they began to exit the plane.

"Where's Allen? I hope he remembered to meet us," Amanda was saying to Jonathan, stretching her neck to see above the crowd.

"I'm sure he'll be here," Jonathan said, moving towards the baggage carousel. Crystal followed Jonathan and noticed a young man waving above the crowd. He was wearing a pair of jeans, a polo shirt, a brown leather jacket and matching cowboy boots. His hair was the colour of prairie wheat. Amanda walked up to him and gave him a quick loose squeeze. Jonathan shook his hand and turned towards Crystal. "This is Crystal, your sister."

"Hi, Sis! Welcome home!" Allen said so instantly and comfortably that Crystal felt she had known him all her life.

"Hi," Crystal said, feeling a bit embarrassed.

Allen smiled and gave her a loose hug. "It's been a while. You'll get used to being back in no time. I'll show you around, so you'll feel more comfortable."

"Allen, I don't think Crystal needs to see the places you're familiar with. I think she should stay around home for a while and get used to being here before you start dragging her around the city," Amanda commented with disgust.

Allen winked at Crystal and turned to Amanda. "Mother, don't be silly. Crystal needs to meet people and get out. We don't want to lock her away, especially in the house with you. That'll drive her right back to where she came from."

Crystal couldn't help but smile at Allen and knew they were going to get along fine. She could tell there was tension between him and Amanda. It didn't seem to bother either of them, or Allen enjoyed bantering with her.

Jonathan returned with the luggage cart, and they exited the airport. Next to the curb sat a black stretch limousine with the door open. A tall, blond-haired man wearing a clean, pressed uniform stood holding the door as Allen jumped in the back.

"I thought I'd bring the limo. Only the best for my little sister," he said, turning and smiling at Crystal.

The surprise was perfectly clear on Crystal's face as they all sat in the back of the limo and the chauffeur closed the door. Allen turned to her. "Let me guess, they didn't tell you. That doesn't surprise me. I'll fill you in on our life when we get home. I don't know how you lived before, but believe me you've hit the big time, baby!"

Amanda spoke up in an offended tone. "Allen, stop that right now! Your father worked his fingers to the bone to build the company into what it is today. You should be proud of his success. You wouldn't have your job if we didn't own the company. Some day, the company will be yours, and with the useless, irresponsible way you behave, it won't be long before you drive it into the ground."

Crystal looked at Jonathan, who sat with his eyes closed and his head leaning back against the black leather seat. He looked tired of everything. He opened his eyes and spoke softly.

"Do you think the two of you could relax for at least the next twenty-four hours until Crystal gets used to us. She's going to wonder what kind of family she's been born into."

Crystal shot him a thankful glance and turned towards the window. Amanda pointed out the Calgary Tower and the Saddledome and made continuous reference to being close to the Rockies. They drove past a sky-scraper covered in glass windows. The lettering above the revolving doors read PEARSON COMPUTERS AND ELECTRONICS CORPORATION.

"This is our company. It's quite different from the small rental space on the outskirts of the city where we started. I couldn't understand Jonathan's interest in computers, but I'm glad he started his own company. It's one of the largest privately owned corporations in Calgary. Once you've settled in, I'll take you on a tour and introduce you to every-one. When you're ready, we'll find a job for you to work here," Amanda said proudly.

"That would be wonderful," Crystal said, trying to fathom the possibilities that were laying themselves at her feet.

"Yeah! You could work in my department. It wouldn't take me long to show you the ropes," Allen interrupted.

"Then you could spend more time on the slopes and the golf course doing absolutely nothing. You're going to have to grow up, Allen, and realize there's more to life than rushing down ski hills and chasing golf balls," Amanda said with scorn.

"I hope not too soon. Don't worry, Mom, I won't disappoint you. Now that Crystal is back, at least you'll have something else to occupy your time instead of focus-ing on what I'm doing and who I'm doing it with," Allen replied jokingly.

"I don't like the people you call friends. They have no direction and no desire to make an honest living. The only way to get anywhere in this life is to work hard for what you want. When you succeed, you can reap the benefits like your father and me," Amanda said, her eyes sparking with fire.

"I don't have to work to reap the benefits, which you continually remind me of," Allen retorted.

"We didn't invest an obscene amount of money into an education for you to have you blow it out a window either," Amanda snapped back.

"Don't worry, Mother. I'm getting an education where it counts. Half of my business deals are achieved over lunch, dinner, on the slopes or on the golf course. I've learned how to maneuver business my own way, and it's been working. If you look at the spreadsheets for this year, you'll see my department is excelling in the profit margins. When my profits start to slip, you'll have a valid reason to get on my case about where I spend my time. For now, let's concentrate on getting Crystal home and being one big happy family." Allen's voice dripped with sarcasm as Crystal listened to the exchange between Allen and Amanda.

The limo began to slow down, and Crystal turned her attention to the window once more. They pulled into a driveway and up to a gate. The driver pressed a button, and a video camera rotated on a pole towards the limo. The huge iron gates began to swing open. The car moved slowly forward as the gates closed behind them.

"Don't worry – you're safe here, Sis. This place is guarded tighter than Fort Knox," Allen said, rolling his eyes.

Amanda shot him a piercing glance. "Allen, that's quite enough of your criticism. Crystal is going to love it here."

The limo came to a stop in front of a stately mansion.

"Wow! This is home?" Crystal exclaimed as she stepped out of the limo and looked at the massive structure before her.

"Thank you, Victor," Amanda said in a condescending manner and walked towards the open door, where a petite young woman with a big, sparkling smile stood waiting for them. Her ebony hair was piled high on the top of her head and held in place by numerous hairpins. Her oval eyes were dark, warm and inviting as she studied Crystal.

"Welcome home, Madam. We have prepared the rooms for Miss Crystal as you instructed," she said as Amanda approached her from the limo.

"Thank you, Maria," Amanda said as she brushed past her into the entryway.

Crystal stepped over the threshold behind Amanda and could hardly believe her eyes. The foyer was Italian marble. There was a long winding oak staircase to the right of where she was standing, and plush teal blue carpet covered the center of the stairs leading to the upper floor of the house.

The hallway that extended before her had white oak hardwood flooring, and family portraits graced the walls that led to beautiful gardens beyond the glass doors at the end. Doorways to mystery rooms broke the uniformity.

"I'd like to freshen up," Crystal said to Amanda and Jonathan.

"That's a good idea, dear. Show her up to her rooms, Maria, and give her a hand getting settled in."

"Yes, Madam. Follow me, Miss Crystal."

Crystal followed Maria up the staircase leading to the second floor. There was a small table at the top of the stairs holding a large vase of fresh cut flowers that filled the hallway with an aromatic floral scent. Crystal followed her down the hallway past closed doors that led to rooms occupied by Amanda and Jonathan. They passed numerous wildlife prints by Glenn Olson, and Crystal stopped to admire one of a mother grizzly and her cubs. Maria opened a door at the end of the hallway.

"These are your rooms," she said, stepping inside. Pointing to her right, she continued, "the bedroom, powder room and facilities are through there. I'll start unpacking for you while you freshen up."

"That's quite all right, Maria. I'm not used to having someone wait on me. I'll unpack myself, thank you," Crystal said dismissively.

Maria nodded and quietly retreated, closing the door behind her.

Crystal ambled through the maze of rooms and looked around. The sitting room held a plush sofa, coffee table, television, and a desk for writing. She walked from the sitting room to the bedroom, where a four-posted, queen-size bed covered with a solid, dark green duvet, matching pillow shams and bed skirt sat against the far wall. A bedside table held the lamp and alarm clock. A massive dresser with a mirror that extended its entire length stood along one wall. Sitting next to it was a full-length wardrobe and ornate armoire. Crystal knew the meager belongings she carried in her suitcases would never fill it. To the far side of the room was a dressing table, lingerie chest and jewelry chest. Crystal entered the bathroom and looked around. In the corner was a jacuzzi tub, a four-by-six walk-in shower with a bench, and a floor-length mirror hung on the back of the door.

She thought of some of the dives she had stayed in. These rooms were bigger than most of the apartments where she and Samuel had lived.

She washed her face and reapplied her makeup. As she looked at herself in the mirror, she wondered exactly who she was. Allen was right. She had hit the big time. She smiled at her reflection and her good fortune, despite the pain that tugged at her heart from leaving Michael and Katie behind. Michael was a simple man with simple tastes. He'd never be comfortable living in a house like this with servants, a chauffeur, and a limo.

She was going to enjoy having the luxuries Amanda and Jonathan seemed so anxious to provide. Allen was rebelling against the wealth and power Jonathan had obtained. If he had grown up like this all his life, not wanting for anything and having whatever he wanted handed to him on a silver platter, he wasn't aware of the hardships of the working class. She knew – boy, did she know – how hard it could be to make ends meet. For now, she would try to look optimistically towards the future. She unpacked her things and returned downstairs.

"How are your rooms? I hope you're satisfied with them," Amanda asked when Crystal returned to the landing.

"Yes, thank you," she replied, not liking the gleam in Amanda's eyes.

"If there's anything you want or need, don't hesitate to call on the staff to get it for you. They're here to take care of us, and they do a particularly good job. We're so glad you're home. I know you'll come to love it here as much as we do. I'm going to take a nap – I'm exhausted from the trip.

If you're not tired, you might want to go out and lounge by the pool until dinner. Feel free to wander around the grounds and familiarize yourself with what's here. In other words, make yourself at home. This is your home now, too," she said, disappearing up the stairs.

Crystal wandered out onto the patio and lowered herself into one of the many lounge chairs lined up along the side of the pool. Closing her eyes, she soaked in the warm streams of sunlight beaming down from the clear blue sky above. This is the life, she thought.

"Can I get you anything, Miss Crystal?" Maria asked, coming up beside her.

"No, Maria, thank you."

"As you wish, Miss," she replied and evaporated as quickly as she had appeared.

"Going for a dip?" Allen's voice called from across the pool.

"No, I'm going to lay here. Why don't you join me? We can catch up."

Maria appeared again. "Can I get you anything, sir?"

"Yes, Maria. A beer, please," Allen said with a smile, and she was gone.

Maria returned with his beer and placed it on the small glass table that sat between them. "Will that be everything?"

"For now, Maria," Allen replied and took a drink from the glass.

"What would you like to talk about?" he asked, looking directly at her.

"Nothing in particular. I thought you might want to tell me about the family and some things about yourself.

To tell you the truth, I don't even remember you. How old are you?"

Allen shifted his position to get comfortable and began to speak. "I'm twenty-six. I head up the programming department at Pearson Computers. I try to improve the old and hire fresh new talent who can develop new software for computer systems.

We're a large operation with small satellite offices around the world. I travel some, but not much. I like staying around here. If there's business to take care of where it's warm, then I go. I like to spend time down south in the winter months. Mother says I party too much and am not serious enough. I tell her I have lots of time to be serious.

When you were kidnapped, we lived across town on the other side of the tracks. Dad opened his own company, and it took off. After a couple of years, they decided to move here. I wasn't allowed out of their sight. They were so nervous about leaving me alone. I had private tutors for school and a bodyguard that followed me everywhere. I didn't have a lot of friends, and I spent most of my time studying. I excelled and finished high school at fifteen. I went to university and graduated with a degree in Business Administration and Computer Sciences. Once I finished, I started the job I have now at Pearson Computers, courtesy of dear ol' Dad. That's it! What about you?"

"Nothing as glamourous as private tutors and university, that's for sure. Samuel, the man who kidnapped me..." Crystal watched Allen nod in acknowledgement. "We moved a lot. Every few months at first. Then, as time went on, we stayed longer in some places, sometimes up to two or three years as I grew older. We lived in trailers, cheap apartments, and motel rooms with housekeeping units. Samuel worked at whatever he could to make ends meet, and sometimes things were tough.

I didn't make a lot of friends in school either because I was moving so much. I studied a lot, too. I took a secretarial course online and was able to get temporary jobs through employment agencies. I was a waitress a time or two at a truck stop. I worked long, hard hours to help Samuel with the bills. He had a drinking problem, which only made matters worse. Then we moved to Corner Brook. I didn't want to see Samuel go to jail, so Amanda gave me a choice. Samuel wouldn't go to jail if I returned with them to Calgary for a year. She didn't like the idea of me living so close to Samuel."

"That sounds like Mother. You liked it where you were?" he asked thoughtfully.

"Yes, very much. Michael and I are in love, and it's the first time I've been in a meaningful relationship. I made friends and would've liked to have stayed."

Crystal enjoyed sitting and talking to him. It was as if they had been friends for years. His easy smile made her comfortable at once, and the sparkle in his eyes was heartwarming. He took another drink from the beer glass and brushed the foam from his upper lip.

"Our lives here are pretty superficial. Things are fine on the surface but perilous underneath. Mother is a domineering woman who will stop at nothing to get what she wants. She watches what happens at Pearson Computers like an eagle surveying its prey. Every move must be justified.

She doesn't trust my capabilities. She's a control freak, and after all the years I've spent in school she doesn't trust my judgement, even though it was me who convinced Dad to go international and expand the technology we produce. He wasn't interested in going any bigger, but with the fast-paced technological advances in the computer world today, we had to expand or be swallowed up by the conglomerates. It's been the best move we ever made, but Mother would never admit it was my idea.

Father, on the other hand, is wonderful. You'll love him. He's chairman of the board and a feisty fellow when it comes to business, but he's not interested in the daily inner workings of the company anymore. He leaves that to Mother. It seems he's lost his drive, and she has enough for both of them. He rarely goes to the office. He has a greenhouse past that stand of trees and spends most of his time out there.

Anyway, you have enough to deal with, without me laying all this family stuff on you your first day here. We'll have lots of time to chat about Ma, Pa, and Pearson Computers. It's good to have you back, Crystal. I was young when you left, but I still missed you."

"I'm sorry I can't say I missed you, too. I don't remember having a brother. Samuel told me I was an only child. I'm glad you're here, though."

Allen finished his beer and stood up. "I have a business dinner this evening. I'd best get ready. I'll leave you to the wolves," he said, winking as he turned and walked inside through the back door.

Crystal got up and stretched. The information Allen had told her about her parents and their company was staggering. She was the daughter of an extremely wealthy, influential businessman. Wait until Michael hears this, she thought. It was like a Cinderella story. She smiled to herself and followed Allen through the door to call Michael. It was hard not having him around, but it was extremely easy to be the guest of Amanda and Jonathan Pearson.

Chapter 5

THE TELEPHONE RANG TWO OR three times before Crystal heard his voice say, "Hello?"

"Michael, it's Crystal. I made it all right. Is Katie home yet?"

"No, she's with Jeremy. How was your flight?"

"It was fine," she replied and told him about her arrival, Allen, the house, and the business Jonathan owned.

"Yes, I know all about Pearson Computers. I did some research before I told you about your parents. I didn't think it was my place to tell you about the company and who your parents were."

Crystal continued to chat with him on the phone. They covered what was happening in Corner Brook. It reminded her of how much she missed him and how much she wanted to be with him. They talked about Samuel and Gloria and how ecstatic they were that the charges had been dropped.

Before she knew it, Maria was knocking on her door to tell her it was time to come down for dinner. She apologized to Michael again for having left, gave him her telephone number at the house and her address, and promised him she would call again soon.

She quickly showered and dressed in a pair of Levi's, a pale aqua shirt, and sneakers before going down to the dining room. She stopped short when she entered. Amanda and Jonathan were sitting there, dressed as if they were going out. Amanda's elegant black dress drained what colour was in her cheeks. She looked almost ghostly. Jonathan was dressed in a navy sports jacket and gray trousers.

The formally laid table was set with sterling silver utensils, bone China, cloth napkins, and pinwheel crystal water glasses and wine goblets. The table was accented with small, perfectly positioned flower arrangements made up of a variety of flowers from the gardens.

Amanda looked at her with disgust on her face. "From now on, would you mind being on time and dressing properly for dinner?" Amanda snapped.

"I'm sorry. I'm not used to dressing for dinner," Crystal said, crossing the dining room floor and sliding into an empty chair, feeling like a chastised child.

Maria began to serve the evening meal of salad, roast chicken, wild rice, and French string beans. The wine was a German white and had a lovely flavour. There was Swiss almond chocolate cheesecake with fresh strawberries for dessert.

Jonathan ate as fast as he could to escape the conversation of the dinner table. Amanda ate poised and proper, taking the time to slowly chew every bite. Once the meal was finished, Jonathan excused himself and disappeared into the maze of the huge house.

"He's always hiding away somewhere. He's either going to that greenhouse of his or to the library. You'd think for your first night home, he'd be available for a bit of evening conversation," Amanda remarked, shaking her head.

"That's quite all right, Amanda. I'm tired. I think I'd be better off with a bath and crawling into bed. It really has been a long day," Crystal said, trying to stifle a yawn.

"Maria, go upstairs and run a hot bath for Crystal," Amanda called in the direction of the kitchen.

"Amanda, it isn't necessary for Maria to wait on me. I find it awkward having her do things for me. If it's all the same to you, I'll wait on myself."

"Nonsense, dear. She's employed by us to look after our needs, and now that you're home, she'll look after yours. I'll not hear of you doing any kind of work around here."

Crystal knew there was no sense in arguing with her and looked at the clock. "What time do you expect Allen home?"

"Not until late. He's out gallivanting with the people he calls friends." Amanda's eyes narrowed.

Crystal picked up her dishes to take them to the kitchen.

"Don't touch those! That's the staff's job," Amanda practically screamed at her.

Crystal put the dishes back on the table. She could understand why Allen spent so little time at home. She was certain she would be approaching Jonathan about a job first thing in the morning. She leaned on the railing of the staircase as she made her way up to her bedroom. The time difference and jet lag, along with the meal and wine were starting to take a toll on her. All she wanted to do was slide into a bathtub full of hot water and then go to bed.

Crystal woke up and found her way to the kitchen. "Good morning, Miss Crystal. What can I get for you this morning?" Maria asked, meeting her in the kitchen doorway.

"Just coffee and a muffin or croissant if you have any, please Maria."

"Hilda made fresh blueberry muffins this morning. Would you like to have breakfast on the patio by the pool or in the dining room?"

"The patio sounds great. Has Allen left for the office already?"

"Allen left early this morning, Miss. He usually leaves before anyone gets up. I'll get your breakfast," she said shyly, her eyes dropping towards the floor.

Crystal sat at the patio table as Maria brought out a silver tray laden with coffee and fresh blueberry muffins. She finished eating and walked towards the path directly behind the house. She walked through an opening in the trees to find an expansive lawn with a large, oblong greenhouse in the middle.

Jonathan appeared from behind the foliage when she opened the door. "Good morning, Crystal. Come on in and look around. This is where I spend most of my time," he explained. "I leave the running of the company to your mother and the rest of the board members. It seems to be better now that I'm just a silent voice behind the scenes. Amanda stays on top of things, and if she feels my input is needed, she lets me know."

Crystal stepped inside and began to wander slowly up and down the aisles of blossoms and greenery. "These roses are beautiful," she said, leaning over to smell one.

"They were your favourite when you were a little girl. We had a rose garden in the back of the old house. You'd get so excited at the sight of the first bud," he said, looking at her with sad, dark eyes.

Crystal gazed at the man who was her father. He was dressed in a white t-shirt and faded denim overalls. He looked like one of the farmers she had seen in some of the towns Samuel and she had lived in. His face wore a soft expression. As he turned toward her, he said in a gentle voice, "I've missed you. I don't want you to think I haven't suffered because of your absence. You were my little princess. I had such plans for you. When you were taken, I buried myself in the company. Amanda continued to look for you, and then became involved in the wheeling and dealing at Pearson.

When Allen finished school, I hoped he would take over. By that time, Amanda was so involved in the running of things there didn't seem to be room for Allen or me. She has become quite a ruthless businesswoman. It seems to have clouded her vision about the importance of family.

Her main concern is outward appearances, and we present ourselves as refined and social equals to the people we deal with. When we found you, I could see you were happy. I tried to talk Amanda out of bringing you back, but she was determined we'd be a whole family again. You add mystery, having the long-lost daughter return to the fold. Do you understand?"

"Yes, Jonathan, I do. I understand fully. I admit I was

happy where I was, and I've been brought up very differently than Allen. I wonder if I'd grown up with you what I'd be like now. But I am who I am. Amanda might not like who her daughter has grown up to be. I know I'm different than what Amanda expects."

He moved cautiously towards her. "I want you to be happy, sweetheart. I haven't said anything to you because I'm a bit afraid you'll disappear again. If you do leave, I'll understand. But we can help you excel in anything you want to do. I'm glad you agreed to come. It'll be nice getting to know you as a woman. Please don't be offended if sometimes I tend to treat you like a little girl. You're still and always will be my little princess."

"I'll remember. One thing I must do is find a job. I'm not used to sitting around all day doing nothing. I like to be busy. I would be happy to start anywhere you can find a spot for me. The mailroom would be fine. I don't want the other employees to think I've received special treatment because I'm the company owner's daughter."

"I'll mention it to Amanda. I'm sure we can put you somewhere." He turned and began to prune and water the roses, indicating to her the conversation was over. He was an incredible man. He was a man you could talk to and spend time with. He was what she had wanted in a father as a child growing up. He understood everything. He said little, but whatever he did say commanded your attention and consideration.

She wandered out of the greenhouse and back towards the pool. She noticed Allen in the kitchen window talking to Maria. As she approached the kitchen, the conversation between them came to an abrupt halt.

Allen looked at her, his eyes sparkling mischievously. "Out getting some fresh air?"

"I was down to the greenhouse. Jonathan certainly has a green thumb. The roses are beautiful."

"Dad and his roses. That's all he thinks about. It's sad really. He has a multi-million-dollar corporation and prefers the thorns of the rose bushes to the battles of the boardroom. Mother has taken over the helm, but he'd do a much better job. He has more finesse when it comes to appeasing clients. Yet he insists on retreating to that flower garden."

"I've asked him to arrange for me to start work," she said, watching Maria, who was silently going about her work in the kitchen.

"You're going to go to work this soon? Fantastic! I could really use you at the office. I need an assistant, and you'd be perfect for the job. What do you say? Want to try it? The job isn't complicated. You could learn it overnight," he said excitedly.

"I wasn't thinking of starting above the mailroom. I don't want any special treatment because I'm the owner's long-lost daughter."

"There's no way Mother will hear of you starting in the mailroom. The only way she'll let you enter the company is in an assistant executive position or directly as an executive. She has standards for her children. It would be best that you learn the ropes quickly or suffer the wrath of Amanda. You'll learn we are not allowed to embarrass her with our actions. She hates to see bad press involving her children or anyone associated with the company. Believe me, I know. We're not ourselves – we are Amanda Pearson's children. We must try no matter how hard it may be to live up to her expectations," he said, rolling his eyes.

"Well, she's going to be completely disappointed in me. I've never had the opportunity to be groomed the way you have. I am who I am. I can't see my personality changing overnight."

"Don't be too sure. She has a way of swiftly turning people into what she wants. Be careful you don't get caught up in the whirlpool. How about I take you down to the office and show you what you'd be doing. Mother will be a bit leery of you starting right away. I'll tell her I need your help. If you're working with me as my assistant, she'll be happy. The position isn't fantastic, but it isn't the mailroom, either."

The conversation in the car on the way to the downtown core of the city focused on what would be expected of her as Allen's assistant. He showed her a bit of the city and pulled the Saab into a reserved parking space in the underground parking lot of the Pearson Computers building. They took the elevator to the executive suites and stepped out into a massive hallway.

"This way," Allen said, turning and leading the way to his office.

They passed secretaries tapping computer keys and switchboard operators answering telephones. People glanced up, smiled, and nodded as Crystal and Allen strolled by. There were original canvas paintings by Robert Bateman hanging on the walls, and Crystal glanced into offices and boardrooms. They stopped at the end of the hall, and a young, attractive blond-haired secretary looked up and smiled at Allen as he approached her desk.

"Good morning, Mr. Pearson. Your messages are on your desk. The report you asked for from Mr. Anderson downstairs is there, too. Can I get you anything?" she asked, eyeing Crystal with curiosity.

"Good morning, Sandra. Yes, coffee please. This is Crystal, my sister. She's going to try her hand at the assistant position we discussed last week at the board meeting."

Sandra smiled at her. "It's a pleasure to meet you, Crystal. I hope you'll enjoy working here. I'll get your coffee, Mr. Pearson."

Sandra was a tall, slender girl in her mid-twenties. She wore a lovely, tailored, jade-green suit that accented her flawless figure. Her long blond hair was loosely captured between her shoulder blades by a barrette that perfectly matched the colour of her suit. Her green eyes had flashed slightly when Allen mentioned Crystal would be his new assistant; her envy was almost completely hidden.

Allen motioned to an office door with a gold-lettered nameplate that read "Allen Pearson, Executive Director, Program Management." Crystal followed him inside and closed the door behind them. His office was decorated in a modern style with chrome and glass. His desk had a smoky glass top and the black leather chair sitting behind it, sat in front of a wall of windows through which you could see the Rocky Mountains.

"This is beautiful, Allen," Crystal said, looking around.

"Have a seat," Allen said, motioning to a large black leather armchair opposite his desk. "I want to check through this stuff, then I'll show you around."

He sat down, sifted through the messages, and separated the paperwork into small piles. The door opened, and Sandra stepped in carrying a silver tray filled with a coffee urn, cups, sugar, and cream. She put the tray on the corner of his desk and smiled sweetly. "Can I get you anything else?"

"No, thanks. These calls must be returned at once. Set up an appointment with Carlos Zambeni and accept his invitation to the dinner party he's holding. I already have other plans for that evening, but you can cancel and reschedule them. Mr. Zambeni's dinner party is far more important. Also, advise them I'll be bringing a guest."

"A guest, Mr. Pearson?" Sandra's surprise was evident.

"Yes, Sandra, I'll be taking Crystal. Mr. Zambeni is one of our most important clients. I would like Crystal to meet him."

"Yes, sir. I'll look after these things immediately," she said, gathering up the different piles of messages and exiting the office.

"Allen, don't you think Sandra would be better for the assistant position?" Crystal asked. "I'm sure she knows more about what you do."

The door opening distracted their attention as Amanda swept unceremoniously into the room.

"Jennifer told me she saw you come in. I was talking to Jonathan on the telephone, and he said Crystal wanted to start work right away. Jennifer said you had a woman with you and described Crystal to a tee."

"Yes, Mother. Your spy was right. She's going to be my new assistant. I thought it best to start her in the assistant position we discussed at last week's board meeting. That way, I'll have more time to concentrate on drawing in clients."

"That's a splendid idea," Amanda replied, beaming. "I'd hoped to start her with me, but being your assistant is fine, too. I'll be right down the hall. She can direct questions to me when you're not in the office. Why don't we leave you to your work? I'll show her around the building. I think the best place to start would be her new office."

Amanda didn't wait for Allen to reply. Crystal stood up and looked apologetically at Allen as Amanda motioned her to follow.

Amanda surveyed the jeans, tank top and sneakers Crystal was wearing and shook her head. "After we're finished here, we'll take you shopping. If you're going to represent this company, you'll need an appropriate wardrobe."

They left Allen's office and entered the empty office next door.

"This should do," Amanda stated, turning towards Crystal.

"This is marvellous, Amanda," Crystal said enthusiastically. "It's more spacious than I would've expected. Most of my bedrooms were never this large."

"You can arrange to have it decorated any way you want. I'll get Jennifer to contact Madeline – she can meet you here in the morning. You can tell her want you want, and she'll see to it."

"Thank you very much," Crystal said excitedly, as she envisioned how she would like her office to look.

"Good, then. Follow me. I'll introduce you to the office staff and have Jennifer arrange for you to have a secretary."

Crystal followed her through the door, feeling like a lady in waiting. This woman commanded respect. Her eyes held no warmth, her dusty rose suit looked stunning as she swayed down the hall, and employees practically bowed as they walked past. Amanda announced, "This is my daughter, Crystal," to everyone they met. They all stopped abruptly to shake her hand and congratulate Amanda for having located her.

Crystal smiled and nodded to everyone to whom she was introduced. Her casual appearance was noted on their faces, and she began to feel self-conscious about the way she was dressed. She watched Amanda's gait and tried to copy her the best she could. Amanda stopped briefly to talk with her secretary, Jennifer, about Madeline meeting with Crystal to decorate her office and the plan to have a secretary hired for her.

"Now, let's see if Allen can join us for lunch. Following that, we'll go shopping," Amanda announced.

They turned around and walked back in the direction of Allen's office.

"Is he free?" she asked Sandra, starting for the door.

"Yes, ma'am," Sandra replied with not even a glance in her direction.

Amanda opened the door, and they went in. Allen looked up from his desk.

"Did she give you the grand tour?"

"Yes, it's quite a place you have here," Crystal replied, chuckling.

Amanda turned to Allen and said, "I'm going to take Crystal to lunch and then shopping. Do you want to come along for lunch?"

"No thanks, Mother. You ladies run along. I have some paperwork to clear up and a business lunch with a few prospective clients."

"Very well. Let's be off," Amanda said, turning to Crystal.

Crystal looked at Allen, who was eyeing her with a sympathetic smile. "Have fun!"

Crystal returned his smile. "I will, thanks," she replied and turned to follow Amanda, who was already walking down the hallway towards the elevator.

They stepped out onto the sidewalk and started to walk downtown. Crystal glanced in the windows of the shops that lined Stephen Avenue, while Amanda watched her closely.

"If you see anything you like, just say so, and we'll stop. Don't worry about the price of anything. Think of this shopping trip as my welcome home present. I never had the chance to take you shopping, so let me enjoy buying you whatever your little heart desires."

They continued downtown, and Amanda motioned towards the entry of a bistro. "Let's have lunch here. The food is fantastic."

"Mrs. Pearson, how wonderful to see you. We were not expecting you today. I'll have your table made ready immediately," the host said politely.

"Thank you. I'd appreciate it," Amanda replied.

As they waited, Crystal watched Amanda nod to patrons having lunch. Crystal looked around and immediately liked the little bistro. The carpets were bright and cheery with a mix match pattern. The tables were glass topped with chrome legs and garden patio style chairs with cushions covering the backs and seats. Plants of every kind hung from the ceiling, and replicas of famous impressionist paintings graced the walls. Black and white uniformed waiters and waitresses scurried silently and efficiently from table to table.

The host returned after a few minutes and ushered them to their table. Placing the menus down on the table in front of them, he looked at Amanda. "Your usual, Mrs. Pearson?"

"Not today. Bring us a bottle of Dom. We're celebrating," Amanda replied, glancing at him.

His eyes widened. "Yes, ma'am."

"This is my daughter. She has just returned home."

"That is a reason to celebrate. I'll get your champagne," the host replied.

"He's such a sweetheart," Amanda said.

"He seems very nice. You obviously come here often," Crystal commented.

"All the time. He knows who I am and appreciates my patronage."

The host returned and poured the champagne into crystal flutes. Amanda ordered their lunches, and they settled in to wait for the meal.

Amanda watched Crystal closely. "This is what you have to look forward to. People will soon realize you're my daughter, and you'll be treated accordingly. Are you enjoying your first couple of days in Calgary?"

"Yes, very much. I could get used to this," Crystal replied, laughing.

Amanda chuckled and nodded. "I noticed an invitation to a dinner party on my desk this morning from Carlos Zambeni. He's one of our biggest clients. I graciously accepted on behalf of Jonathan and myself. I also added your name to the guest list. You'll like Carlos. He's of Italian and South American descent and is involved in the modeling industry. He's extremely wealthy, and he's single."

"Amanda, I'm in love with Michael, and when my year is up, I intend to return to Corner Brook to be with him. Allen has already advised Mr. Zambeni that I'll be attending as his new assistant."

"Oh, that's wonderful. You can mix business with a bit of pleasure, and as far as Michael is concerned, I don't see any harm in having a bit of fun while you're staying here with us."

The food arrived, and they busied themselves with the meal. Crystal couldn't pronounce the seafood dish Amanda ordered, but it was flavourful and seemed to melt in her mouth. They finished their lunch, and Amanda left a generous tip. She reminded the host that he should treat Crystal the same as he would her. He listened carefully to Amanda and reassured her that the instructions would be followed exactly. He would see to it that all employees were made aware of her wishes.

They spent the afternoon in dress shops, shoe stores, and accessory shops. Crystal picked up a few things for Michael and Katie. It was fun not having to look at the price tag or worry about the total when getting the receipt.

Following their afternoon outing, they returned to the office. Crystal wandered towards Allen's office where Sandra advised her that he had left for the day. She went back to Amanda's office to wait until Amanda was ready to leave. Jennifer ushered her inside and motioned for her to sit down.

The office was typical of any corporate executive. There was an old-fashioned wooden desk against one wall with a lovely Robert Bateman canvas, Shadow of the Rainforest, hanging behind it. The desk faced a full glass wall through which you could see the snow-capped Rocky Mountains looming in the distance on a sunny day. There were plants hanging and sitting on the floor, filling in the empty corners. Modern art pieces decorated the tables, and a large Roman statue stood next to a small bar. The whole office screamed wealth and power.

Amanda talked sternly on the telephone as Crystal sat waiting. She could see Amanda was distressed about something. She ended the conversation sharply and slammed the receiver into its cradle.

"People think sometimes that because you're a woman, they can take advantage of you. Don't ever let them do that to you, Crystal. Let them know what you want and demand they give it to you."

Amanda stood up and walked around the desk, stretching. "Let's call it a day, shall we? You can start working in the morning. I'm sure Hilda has something fabulous planned for dinner. I'm starving."

The next couple of weeks flew by. Crystal enjoyed the job, and it seemed to come naturally to her. There was a lot to learn, and Amanda hovered over her. Allen helped when he wasn't out drumming up business. When she returned home in the evenings, all she wanted to do was eat and crawl into bed.

She was adjusting to being wealthy better than she thought. Even Michael's voice was growing distant when she talked to him on the phone. She hadn't been in touch with him much. There never seemed to be enough time now that she was working. When she had a chance to call him, the time difference between Alberta and Newfoundland created another problem.

He was busy in his world, and she was busy in hers. The last time they spoke, the conversation was strained, and there was tension growing between them. She knew she was changing. Amanda arranged for her to have expense accounts throughout the city and introduced her to everyone she knew. They were astonished by the long-lost daughter story. People were pleasant and seemed to be delighted to accept her into their social circle.

Chapter 6

ON THE NIGHT OF CARLOS Zambeni's dinner party, the Pearson family arrived presenting a united front at the gala affair. Jonathan and Allen looked stunning in their black tuxedos, and Amanda was the stately matriarch dressed in a gorgeous, ivory satin gown. She had picked out a black, strapless, floor-length dinner dress for Crystal and bought a thick rope of diamonds that sparkled at her throat. Matching earrings glittered beneath the loose strands of hair that fell from the crown of braids encircling her head.

Amanda spent the first few minutes pointing out important clients to Crystal and explaining who they were to her. Allen disappeared, and Jonathan stood beside Amanda silently. He looked extremely uncomfortable, and Crystal felt sorry for him. Amanda had insisted he attend. Crystal could still hear her voice penetrating through the doors of the mansion's great hall. "Jonathan, you must attend. Carlos is one of our most valued clients. It would be absolutely unforgiveable if you didn't go."

Crystal was thankful Amanda stayed close. She introduced her to the men and women who approached the three of them. Jonathan nodded cordially. Through the crowd, Crystal noticed a tall, dark-complected man dressed in a white tuxedo smiling at her. She held her breath as he started walking towards them. With a gleaming smile, he approached Amanda and Jonathan, while concentrating on Crystal.

Taking Amanda's hand, he kissed the back of it tenderly, and with a voice that held a heavy accent he asked, "Is this your daughter I've been hearing so much about lately?"

"Yes, Carlos. This is Crystal," Amanda replied, smiling.

"Crystal, Mr. Carlos Zambeni, owner of Zambeni Modeling."

"How do you do? It's a pleasure to make your acquaintance," she stammered.

"The pleasure is all mine. Please call me Carlos – all my friends do. I hope once the music starts, you'll honour me with a dance."

"I'd be happy to," Crystal replied.

"I'll hold you to that. Now, if you'll excuse me, I must continue greeting my guests," he said with a twinkle in his eyes.

Carlos had clean features, high cheekbones, and short black hair. His dark eyes danced with mischief, and his smile was dazzling. He was tall and lean, and as she watched him walk away his gait radiated confidence, power, and wealth.

"He seemed to be quite taken with you." Amanda's voice

interrupted her thoughts. "He's one of the best catches around. He's powerful, wealthy, extremely handsome, single, and his company is renowned throughout the world for providing some of the world's most beautiful models. I don't know where he finds them. His models are unique and have been on the covers of the most popular magazines. I've heard he has real estate holdings worldwide, and travels to every nook and cranny of the globe scouting talent for his company."

Carlos returned shortly after the music started and asked Crystal to dance. He expertly glided her around the floor. He spoke of his modeling company and his global travels. His eyes watched her closely, and she felt uncomfortable under his gaze. When the music stopped, he returned her to Amanda and Jonathan's side. The evening seemed to fly by, and before she knew it, they were leaving.

As they prepared to go, Carlos walked up to Crystal. "I'd like to get to know you better, Crystal. Could we have lunch this week or dinner if your schedule allows it? Maybe both? I'll have my secretary call yours and make the arrangements. Is that all right with you?"

"That sounds wonderful, Carlos. I'll look forward to it," she said, shooting him her best smile.

As they left, Allen began to tease her mercilessly. "Looks like you really captivated him, little sister. Everyone was abuzz with how he paid more attention to you than anyone else. Of course, the man isn't blind, and you look breathtaking tonight. Clearly the most beautiful woman in the room. All the men I talked with wanted to know who the new mystery beauty was with Carlos. Your date calendar is going to become extremely busy – I can practically guarantee it."

Amanda looked like the cat that swallowed a canary. Jonathan looked relieved the party was over. He sat and laid his head against the leather seat of the limo as they drove away. He looked tired and worn. Crystal wondered if he was well.

"Whatever your schedule is this week, darling, clear it for Carlos. We don't want to offend him. We're trying to convince him to move all his contracts to our firm. Be sure you're free when he calls," Amanda instructed her.

"Yes, Amanda. But once he gets to know me, he'll realize I'm not as glamourous as the women he normally encounters."

"Maybe that's exactly what he's looking for in someone to settle down with."

Carlos called, and Crystal found herself being wined and dined in a way she had only imagined. He sent overflowing bouquets of flowers to her office and began calling her two and three times daily. They were quickly becoming an item. Amanda was ecstatic with the turn of events, and Crystal felt like she was living a dream. Carlos escorted her to dinners and company functions. He took her to expensive restaurants and surprised her by not encouraging a physical relationship. He was a gentleman, and she began to forget about Michael and Katie.

Carlos and Crystal had been seeing each other nonstop when one evening while they were having dinner in the Calgary Tower, Carlos asked Crystal to leave Pearson Computers and come work for him. He said he wanted to teach her the modeling business. He thought she might have a pulse on what might be the next new look, a fresh and younger view on modern clothing style trends. He was departing on a month-long excursion to look for new modeling talent and wanted her to join him. When Crystal mentioned it to Amanda, she was very agreeable.

"Go, my dear. Carlos is a master in his trade. It's a chance of a lifetime. We'll miss you at Pearson, but you've definitely made an impression on Carlos. If a permanent relationship develops, it could be the merger of the century. Who knows who you'll meet and how it might benefit Pearson Computers?"

When she told Michael of her plans, he was not so understanding. Crystal could hear traces of anger in his voice. "What do you know about this guy? You can't go gallivanting around the world with a stranger."

"Michael, Carlos is a perfect gentleman," she almost shouted into the receiver.

"Crystal, you have no experience with men like him. They draw women in, buy them expensive presents, take them on extensive world tours, buy them jewelry and offer them all kinds of things. Then they discard them like yesterday's trash. He'll hurt you. Men like Carlos are used to owning women. You're just a new trinket in his collection."

"Michael, don't be ridiculous. After all, you deceived me, didn't you? Your interest in me began as an investigation into my past," she said, becoming increasingly upset. The telephone line went silent, and she was instantly sorry for what she'd said.

"Carlos is hiring me to do a job. Travelling around the world is part of that job. I've only dreamed of the places we'll be going. Once the initial trip is over, I'll have an assistant and I'll be traveling with her. It's the opportunity of a lifetime for me, and it's one I'm going to take. It could be also very beneficial for Pearson Computers. Amanda is all for me leaving the company and working for Carlos," she said, softening her tone of voice.

"Crystal, where do we go from here? Have you changed your mind about coming back? Is there any future for us?" Michael's voice became a whisper, and she strained to hear him on the other end of the telephone line.

These were questions she didn't want to answer. For the past few weeks, she had been turning them over in her mind. Where did Michael and Katie fit into her new life?

"I'm not sure anymore, Michael. My life has changed. I'm not the person I was when I left Newfoundland," she said, trying to steady her voice.

Michael's voice began to quiver. "Crystal, go and do everything you want to do. Good luck in your new position and enjoy your trip. I don't think it's wise for you to call anymore. Once the decision has been made, it's not a good idea to look back. I hope you'll be happy. Take care of yourself. Goodbye, Crystal," he said and hung up the telephone.

Crystal replaced the receiver in its cradle and stared at the fire crackling in the fireplace of the living room. She took a sip of wine; it was over, really over. She felt a knot form in the pit of her stomach. Michael had been her first love. Now they were living in two different parts of the country and two different worlds.

Michael was a small-town police officer going nowhere and not wanting to. She was involved in the corporate world now. Doors were opening for her that she thought were far beyond her reach when she was living in filthy, dingy apartments with Samuel. She was in a world where she could have everything she wanted. She would hold a position in Carlos's agency and travel around the world. Nothing was impossible. It was a heady feeling. I'll get over Michael, she thought as she finished her wine.

The telephone rang again, and she swiftly picked up the receiver, hoping it was Michael calling back to apologize and tell her he had changed his mind.

"Crystal, darling, how are you?" Carlos's heavy accent came across the line.

"Fine, Carlos."

"I called to see if you've made up your mind," he said, his voice sounding hopeful. "I'm sorry to rush you, but I don't want to go away and leave you behind. I've become extremely fond of you, and I'll miss you if I have to go alone." His voice changing to a smooth, sexual tone. "Please say you've decided to join me. I'll show you all the points of interest. It will be a pleasure and business trip. I promise you'll enjoy yourself. It will be a way for you to see how my business is run. Plus, you'll get to meet interesting people and see every aspect of what I do for a living."

"When you put it that way, Carlos, how can I refuse? I was worried about how Amanda would feel about me leaving the company, but she's all right with it. My answer is yes. I hope you won't be disappointed with your decision," she said, pushing Michael from her thoughts.

"I'm a great judge of character. Don't worry, you'll do fine. I've assigned you an assistant, and you'll find her invaluable. After this trip, you and she will do my traveling for me. Of course, I'll be coming along from time to time. Ava has been working for me for over five years. She is extremely professional and will be able to teach you everything you need to know. One of our biggest problems is the transportation of the designer clothing worn by the models. Ava is well-known by customs officials and travels between countries with ease. You'll learn from her how to talk and collaborate with the officials to make the transition from country to country relatively quick and easy."

"That's wonderful, Carlos. I was beginning to wonder how I was going to manage traveling through so many countries. I've never been outside of Canada."

"Do you own a passport? We'll be leaving at the beginning of next week," Carlos inquired, concerned.

"Yes. Amanda arranged for me to get one immediately after I arrived in case I wanted to travel with Allen."

"Crystal, I'm glad you're coming with me. This job will be perfect for you. We're going to make a wonderful team," Carlos said affectionately.

"Yes, Carlos, I agree. I think we'll make a wonderful team," she replied, hanging up the telephone.

Crystal poured herself another glass of wine and sat curled up on the sofa watching the fire, engrossed in her own thoughts. Her life had changed so much. There was Michael and Katie, the uncovering of her past, meeting her biological family, the trip to Calgary, a fantastic job with her family's company and now Carlos.

She thought about Michael and Katie back in Newfoundland. Their lives were so different from what she had experienced in Calgary. They were so far removed from the rest of the world. Michael didn't seem to understand the need she had to make something of herself and be recognized in the corporate world as a member of her family. She thought about the comments he'd made earlier about her inexperience. I'll show him, she thought. I'll show him I can do this.

She thought about Katie and how hurt and disappointed she would be when Michael told her she wasn't returning. She was a delightful little girl. She deserved a mother who was happy staying at home. Crystal wanted everything Amanda and Carlos could give her. It scared her to think of how she had changed since her move to Calgary. Her eyes were being opened to a whole new world.

A light tap on the door casing made her jump slightly. Allen stood there, and it was clear he had been drinking by the redness in his eyes and the disarray of his clothing.

"Crystal, Mother told me you were leaving the company to work for Carlos. Are you really going to leave?" he asked, his voice slightly slurred.

"Yes, Allen, I am. In fact, I just got off the phone with Carlos. I discussed the matter with Amanda earlier today. She was thrilled with the position he's offered me. To be quite honest, I'm excited about it myself."

Allen entered the sitting room and dropped down on the sofa. He glanced around the room and then spoke. "Do you think I could bother you to mix me a drink? I'm not very steady on my feet this evening, it seems."

Crystal walked to the small bar sitting in the corner of the room.

"What can I get you?" she asked, taking a glass from the shelf.

"Scotch and water will do nicely, thanks."

She poured his drink, refilled her wine goblet, and handed Allen his glass.

"Crystal, you don't know Carlos Zambeni. I should've talked to you earlier. I thought this little romance wouldn't last. When Mother told me you were leaving the company to move to his firm, I had to talk to you," he said in a slurred voice that held more than a note of concern.

"What are you trying to say, Allen?"

"Carlos is a very powerful man, and little happens without his knowing. There've been rumours that people have paid dearly for going against his orders or crossing him. He guards his actions, and nothing has ever been linked to him. There've been questions raised about his activities and the people he associates with. Are you following me?"

"No, I don't think I am. Carlos has always been the perfect gentleman with me. He's extremely polite, and if you're concerned about our relationship, don't be. Carlos and I are getting along famously. We're quite a good fit for one another. He's a very private man when it comes to business. He's explained that he has to be careful who he trusts. I must admit, his moods and the bodyguards who follow us have made me a bit nervous, but Carlos assures me the guards are there for our safety. He's a man who takes precautions."

"Crystal, think about it. Don't you think it's odd that he's become so involved with you? I'm not saying you're beneath him. I don't think you are, but he's offering you a high-profile job in an agency he's built from the ground up. He has thousands of experienced people that could do the work you'll be doing."

"Allen, Carlos has complete faith in my ability, and besides, didn't you take a big risk in hiring me? Sandra would have been far better suited for the job."

"Crystal, you're family. That's different."

"Well, Allen, thank you for your vote of confidence. I think you've had too much to drink and for whatever reason have had a difficult day and have decided to take it out on me. Amanda seems to be the only one who's happy for me. Jonathan has expressed concern but has given me his blessing. I'd appreciate that from you, too."

"Crystal, I'm sorry. It's not that I think you can't do the job. I'm sure you can. As far as Mother is concerned, she's excited, yes. She's hoping for a merger between you and Carlos personally – that way, the firms will be connected, and she can plan a company merger. Mother only has the company's interests in mind. She would agree to you and Carlos becoming a united couple if you get my drift. If you and Carlos were to marry, she would approach the subject of the firms uniting. We'd be one of the most powerful privately owned companies in Canada, and our software could be used in all his businesses. It would be a huge boost to our bottom line and what we may be able to achieve worldwide."

"Allen, I'm not planning a wedding anytime soon, so Amanda may be disappointed. I'm planning to work for Carlos, to travel with him and learn everything I can. I'm looking forward to seeing places I've only read about." Crystal stood up, signalling an end to the conversation.

Allen gulped the remainder of his drink and stood up, steadying himself with the arm of the sofa.

"Please be careful, Crystal. That's all I'm asking. Keep your eyes open for anything unusual. If you suspect anything, promise you'll get out fast."

"I'm not quite sure what you mean, and I think your concerns are a bit dramatic," she said, resting her hand on his arm reassuringly.

As she went to leave the room, she noticed Maria coming down the hall. Maria walked up and took Allen by the arm. "I'll help him to his room, Miss Crystal."

Over the next week, all Crystal could think about was traveling with Carlos. Amanda helped her pick out the clothing she would need. They would be traveling to London, Paris, Berlin, and Rome. Carlos had told her the next trip would include Scandinavia, the Middle East, and East Asia. Unfortunately, he wouldn't be accompanying her. By that time, he said, she'd be able to manage things on her own with Ava's assistance.

Allen remained distant and Jonathan said little, as usual. Amanda dismissed their reactions, saying they had no faith in the abilities of women in business and were just upset because Crystal was leaving the company to work for Carlos. When Crystal confided in Amanda the concerns Allen had voiced in their conversation, her eyes hardened.

"Allen has always been jealous of Carlos. He's a thorn in Allen's side. Carlos has connections and business partners Allen would love to penetrate but can't. Allen is good at what he does, and it's because of what he does that we're one of the best in the business. However, Carlos has never given us his full contracts. Allen has been unable to convince him we're the firm for all his computer needs in his business ventures. Now, Carlos has taken his little sister from the family business. Allen being upset is only natural. Don't worry, sweetheart, Allen will get over it. You'll have a wonderful time aboard with Carlos. You go and enjoy yourself. Don't concern yourself with Allen. He normally talks out of turn anyway, especially when he's drinking. He's never been one to exercise any kind of tact."

Carlos came by the house to pick her up the morning of their departure. When she settled herself into the back of the limo, she looked across the aisle at a beautiful auburn-haired young woman about her age with bright blue eyes. She was dressed in a simple, elegant, navy-blue business suit. Her skin looked smooth as silk, and she had a sensuous mouth that spread into a full smile revealing perfect pearl-white teeth.

"Hi, Crystal. I'm Ava, your assistant. I've been looking forward to meeting you. Carlos told me you're nervous about traveling into foreign countries. I'll oversee all the traveling arrangements and deal with the customs officials. I've been in and out of so many countries, I've lost track."

"I was nervous until Carlos told me about you," Crystal replied.

They boarded a private jet and were in the air within minutes. Crystal sat back and relaxed. The jet was equipped with everything imaginable. There was a waiter serving drinks and hors d'oeuvres. There were telephones ringing and secretaries busily jotting down messages. It was like Carlos had moved his entire office onto the jet. It was hard to believe they were thirty-five thousand feet above the ground zooming towards London.

After landing at Heathrow, Ava spoke to the customs officials, and they were processed immediately. A steel-gray Rolls Royce pulled up as they came out of the building. The porter loaded the luggage, and they were soon driving towards the hotel. Carlos instructed the driver to detour around Buckingham Palace, Big Ben, and Piccadilly Circus. Crystal sat glued to the window as they sped by.

Carlos smiled. "It's a beautiful city. I'll show you as much as I can while we're here. For now, we must get settled and have dinner. You have a big day tomorrow."

The Rolls Royce pulled up in front of the Mandrake Hotel. "Welcome back, sir. We're happy to see you back in London," the valet said, opening the door of the Rolls.

The porter showed Crystal to her room, where she unpacked, showered, redid her makeup, and changed her clothes. Instead of going out for dinner, Carlos decided he would take her downstairs to the hotel dining room.

When they were seated, Carlos ordered a glass of scotch for himself and a glass of white wine for her. While they waited for their drinks to arrive, Carlos explained the points she should look for when assessing women. He said they'd be lucky to find two women out of all the young women they would see who suited his client. Carlos had made plans to be in London a week before continuing to Paris.

He had rented a cottage outside the city, and they would go there alone for a day or two to relax and review the candidates. Ava would contact the women and arrange for their travels to Canada. The entire process was exciting for Crystal. She began surveying the women occupying the nearby tables.

There wasn't only their outside beauty to consider or the way they dressed, but also little things like the way they sat, their body movements, and the look in their eyes. These were things the public didn't notice but were important. When they were modeling, people were concentrating on their beauty and how they were dressed, yet subconsciously the other points were making an impression. She listened carefully to Carlos explaining all the details.

"I'm not qualified for this. I don't know what's important and what's not," she said nervously to Carlos.

"Don't worry. Ava will be with you when I'm not, and she has a keen eye. It won't be long before you develop the same talent. I'm rarely wrong in my business affairs, and from the moment we met I knew you'd be perfect for this type of work. Trust me, darling – before you know it, you'll be looking at people very differently. Once you're familiar with what we require in women, you'll start learning the key factors in what would make a male model appealing," he said reassuringly.

Carlos ordered their meal, and they decided to leave business behind them for the remainder of the evening. He was interested in hearing about Samuel, Michael, and growing up on the move. He listened closely without interrupting. It felt good for her to be able to talk to him. There hadn't been anyone since Michael whom she felt close to. She began to relax, enjoying the atmosphere of the restaurant and the feeling of the wine. She finished her story and said, "That's it, in a nutshell."

Carlos nodded. "It's been a hard couple of months for you. It must be a tremendous change having moved from Corner Brook to Calgary. Do you plan to return to Newfoundland once your year is complete in Calgary?" he questioned. "This Michael seems to have been an important part of your life."

"Yes, he was, but my time with Michael Blackburn is over, and now it's time to move on," she stated with finality.

"Michael Blackburn? I know of a Michael Blackburn. He worked with the Canada Security Intelligence Service in Ottawa about three or four years ago," Carlos said thoughtfully.

Crystal started to laugh. "Michael is a small-town cop. He heads up a division on missing children, runaway teens, that sort of thing. He's not the type to be a big-time CSIS agent or anything like that."

"I'm glad to hear you're going to stay. I'd hate to think of you leaving soon. You'd find it hard to continue working in this field from Corner Brook. With our work, you need immediate access to all the major cities of the world. Sometimes, you'll find yourself flying at a moment's notice. It might be wise to keep a set of luggage packed on a continual basis so you're always ready to go.

Florida is another place where I have business interests. Our stays in Miami are brief but nonetheless frequent. We also travel round trip from Miami to New York, Chicago, Detroit, and Los Angeles about once a month. Our travel is primarily around North America, but occasionally we look internationally for a certain type of model. This only happens once every four to six months. The travel schedule is exhausting and intense. Are you sure you'll be able to manage it?"

"Yes, oh yes! If there's anyone who knows how to move on short notice it's me, whether it's five hundred miles or five thousand. That's about the only requirement I'm truly qualified for," Crystal said enthusiastically

They left the restaurant and walked to the elevator. He put his arm around her, and she relaxed her head against his shoulder as the floors ticked by. When the elevator stopped, they made their way to the penthouse.

"I had such a wonderful time tonight, Carlos," she sighed.

"So did I, Crystal. So did I," he cooed.

Carlos unlocked the door, and they entered his penthouse suite. The people that had been there earlier had all disappeared. There was a fire burning in the electric fireplace and a bottle of champagne on the coffee table chilling in an ice bucket. He broke the seal, and the cork popped. She jumped slightly and giggled. Carlos smiled and nodded his head towards the bottle. "Would you like a nightcap, or do you want to retire for the evening?"

"I'd love a glass, thank you," she said, even though she was starting to feel giddy from the wine at dinner.

Carlos poured the sparkling liquid and sat on the sofa close to Crystal. Leaning towards her, he placed his arm around her shoulder and raised his glass. "Welcome to my organization, Crystal. I hope your stay is a pleasant one."

"Thank you," she said, raising her champagne flute to meet his.

Carlos gazed deeply into her eyes. "If I'm moving too fast for you, Crystal, just say so," he whispered in her ear.

She sat silent, her body tingling all over. Carlos kissed her sensuously on the mouth, his hand gently removing the glass from hers. She placed her arms around his neck returned his kiss, leaning into him.

The electric fire continued to cast a romantic glow in the room as Carlos expertly removed the clasps in her hair, letting it fall freely around her shoulders and down her back. He meticulously began to unbutton her blouse while continually caressing her and kissing her lightly around her neck and shoulders.

"You're so beautiful," he whispered, passion building in his throat.

Her clothes seemed to magically disappear, and Carlos began to undress himself. When he took off his shirt, Crystal's eyes rested on one of the most horrific scars she had ever seen.

He noticed her surprise. "One of the little mementos I picked up after moving to this country. I was mugged in Vancouver. It was a flesh wound – it looks worse than it was. Does it bother you?"

"No, not at all. It was just a surprise, that's all," she stuttered, not wanting to hurt his feelings or spoil the mood.

Carlos continued to remove his clothes and rejoined her on the sofa. She felt clumsy and inadequate, finding it hard to relax as Carlos began to fondle her breasts and gradually move his hand between her legs. As his passion began to grow and his breathing became laboured with desire, he laid her backwards and entered her forcefully. His rhythm became rapid, and she struggled to keep up. Moments later, she felt him shudder and his body go limp.

"That was wonderful, darling. We're going to make an

incredibly good team indeed," he said between heavy gasps for air.

He stood up and took a long drink of champagne, emptying his glass. Then, sweeping his clothes from the floor, he moved toward an open door to the left of where they sat.

"The washroom is through here."

Crystal stood up, gathered her clothes, and followed Carlos. As she dressed, a strange feeling descended over her. When she returned, Carlos was sitting on the sofa in a white terrycloth hotel bathrobe.

"I poured you another glass of champagne," he said, nodding in the direction of the coffee table.

"I don't think so, Carlos. I'm beginning to feel the effects of the flight and the alcohol. I'm going to go to my room. We have a big day ahead of us tomorrow. I want to make sure I'm alert and ready to go. I hope you're not upset."

"No, darling, not at all. I understand what the time difference and jetlag can do to the body. You run along. I'll see you in the morning. Good night, Crystal," he said, turning his attention to a stack of papers on his desk.

Crystal left and walked to her room. She poured herself a glass of water and went into the bathroom to take a shower. The hot water ran over her as she stepped in, and her body began to relax.

She washed, dried herself off, and strolled back into the bedroom. She pulled on her chemise and slid between the sheets trying to shake off the feeling of emptiness. She curled up and closed her eyes, pulling the covers closer around her chin.

Michael, I miss you so much, she thought and wiped away the tears that slid down her cheek, landing on the pillow.

Chapter 7

THE EARLY MORNING SUN BEAMED brightly as Michael sat on his deck with a hot cup of coffee staring into space. He glanced over into the bare backyard of the bungalow next door. The house was empty and quiet. No one had come to rent it since Crystal and Samuel had moved out. He pictured Crystal walking out and waving.

He was disgusted with himself for the argument they had had on the phone. If he had swallowed his pride and called back right away, he wouldn't have had the conversation with the maid, Maria. She told him that Crystal was out of the country for a month. He inquired if it was with Pearson Computers, and Maria said Crystal could be reached through Carlos Zambeni at Zambeni Modeling.

Then, when he called, the secretary had told him Crystal was on a business trip and was not expected back until the end of the month. She would be delighted to forward a message, but he declined and hung up. These past couple of days, Michael had done nothing but think about Crystal, where she was, and who she was with. Sitting there that morning, he knew what he had to do. He went to the telephone and dialed. His mother's voice cheerily answered on the other end.

"Mom, it's Michael. How've you been?"

"Fine, Michael. It's so good to hear from you. What's wrong, honey? I can tell by your voice something is wrong. Is it Katie? Are you all right?"

"I need your help," he said cautiously.

"Anything, honey."

"I need you to take Katie for a while."

"I'd love to, for as long as you need. Are you in trouble again? What's happening? Is she all right?" Her voice sounded excited and then quickly changed to concern.

"We're fine. I'm assigning myself to an involved investigation. I'm going to have to travel. I don't want to leave Katie with a sitter for an indefinite period of time." Michael tried to sound unconcerned.

"What kind of investigation? Is it dangerous?"

"I'm hoping it's not. If it turns out that way, I want to know Katie is safe."

"Where are you going, Michael?" "I'm going to Ottawa for background information and to contact a few old friends. Then, I'm flying to Calgary, where I think this investigation will take off. I'm not sure where it's going to lead me from there, if anywhere. I want Katie to be with you. I have a few loose ends to tie up here, and then Katie and I will fly to Halifax. I'll drive her up before flying to Ottawa. I'll make the arrangements and let you know when to expect us."

"That's fine, sweetheart. I'll be delighted to have her here. We'll have a wonderful time and, believe me, you and I will talk further when you get here."

"Yes, Mom. I'll tell you everything when I arrive," he said, returning the receiver to its cradle.

The police station was busy. Michael nodded to a couple of his colleagues on his way to Captain Steward's office. He knocked on the glass window and waited until he was told to enter.

The captain looked up and closed a file as Michael walked in and closed the door.

"Blackburn, what's up?"

"Tom, I need a favour," Michael said, sitting down in the chair opposite him.

"What can I do for you?"

Tom liked Michael. He was a good cop and had a way with people Tom hadn't seen in a long time. When Michael joined his force, Tom thought he would be bored. He'd had such an auspicious career and extensive background, but he needed a place to get out of the intense investigations he had been involved in. He'd asked to transfer to the police force in Corner Brook, and Tom was happy he had done so. He had been lucky to get him. Michael reassured him that being a small-town police officer was exactly what he needed. It hadn't taken Tom long to realize Michael had been right.

"I need an extended leave of absence. I have to go out of town for a while. I'm not sure how long I'll be gone. I don't want to lose my job here, but this is something I must do."

Tom studied Michael. Tom could tell he was serious. This was something important to Michael and he was determined to do it, with or without his consent.

"Are you in trouble, Michael? Is there anything I can do to help?"

"No. It's personal. I'd rather not go into it, if you don't mind."

"What are you going to do with Katie? Are you taking her with you? Is she all right?"

"Katie is fine. I'm taking her to stay with my mother. Are you going to let me go?"

"You know I will. I'm going to miss you but go and do what you need to do. Your job will be here when you get back. What are you going to do with the cases you're working on?"

"Dan has agreed to take them over for me. He and I have been working closely for the past year. He's familiar with my caseload, and he's the most qualified."

"Yes, you're right. When are you leaving?"

"As soon as I can."

"If you need anything, don't hesitate to call. I hope you can settle whatever it is. I want your word you'll be back. I don't want to lose you to another police force."

"Don't worry, Tom – I'll be back. You have my word on that," Michael said, extending his hand across the desk.

"Take care of yourself, Michael, and good luck. We'll look forward to your return."

Michael left the station and returned home to pack. His head began to spin with the things he needed to do.

He had to talk to Katie. She'd be happy about visiting her grandmother. She loved the farm in Nova Scotia. He picked up Katie and told her about visiting and staying with her grandmother while he was away. Michael could see the look of excitement in the little girl's eyes.

"When do we leave?" she asked, bouncing up and down on the passenger's seat beside him.

"We're leaving first thing in the morning. I have everything packed."

"Are you going to get Crystal, Dad?" she asked, quickly becoming serious.

"I'm going to try, sweetheart. I'm going to visit her and try to talk her into coming home. I don't want you to get your hopes up."

"If anyone can get her to come back, it's you, Dad. I know you can. I miss her so much."

"I miss her too, Katie. That's why I'm going to visit her. You'll be good for Gramma Virginia?"

"Oh yes. I can't wait to see her. I hope Midnight remembers me. Do you think he will?"

Midnight was Katie's little black Shetland pony his mother kept at the farm for her. It had been a present after the death of Katie's mother. The pony had helped distract her from the loss of her mother.

"How could Midnight forget you?" Michael replied.

Michael gave Katie her supper, and then tucked her into bed for the night. He went into the study, poured himself a whiskey and water and dialed the telephone.

"Yeah," came booming through the line.

"Ed, it's Michael Blackburn. How've ya been?"

"Michael? Michael Blackburn! How the hell are you? Are you in town?"

"No, not yet. I'm flying in Friday evening. Can we get together?"

"Sure! What time do you arrive? I'll pick you up at the airport."

"I get in about eight-thirty in the evening. I'll text you the details. Are you sure it's not a problem to meet me? I can get a cab and meet you later."

"Don't mention it. Where are you staying? You can bunk here if you want. Martha would love to see you."

"No, thanks. I've got things to do. I won't be in town long."

"Michael, this isn't a pleasure trip, is it? What's going on? Thinking about coming back?"

"Not on your life. I like what I'm doing. It's nice being away from it all. I'll explain everything Friday night."

"Yeah, all right. It'll be great to see you, Michael. Things haven't been the same since you left."

"See you Friday, Ed," Michael said, hanging up the phone.

Ed Billings was one of the best friends Michael had at CSIS. He had been the director when Michael was working there as an undercover agent. He was a gentle giant. He towered over everyone at the office and was continually tracking his agents. He was hefty, but athletic, and his hands were the size of bear paws. He was bald, and his deep blue eyes made you feel like he could see right through you. He had an intuitional knack for identifying when someone was beating around the bush. He was the first to offer Michael an undetermined amount of time off following the incident. Ed knew Michael was burnt out and needed to get away. He had Katie to think about and protect, and he knew nothing was more important to him than her.

Michael sat back and thought about Crystal. She had been gone too long. He missed her. He missed their long conversations, her laugh, and her smile. He had felt the same way when his wife died. The house seemed empty, bare, and lifeless.

He was going to try to convince her to return home. But first he had to know what he was up against. This guy Carlos sounded suspicious. He wanted to check things out before moving on to Calgary. That's why he'd called Ed. Ed knew him and his history, and he'd been a real friend, but most of all Michael trusted him.

Michael drained his glass and went to bed. Things would fall into place eventually, and there was no use trying to plan his next step without getting the facts first.

On the flight to Halifax, Katie amused herself by chatting with the other passengers until she tired herself out and went to sleep. Michael looked down at her. Her dark hair zigzagged around her face, and she twisted and moaned in her seat. His mother would be thrilled to have her stay. She had offered to keep Katie permanently after his wife died, but Michael had refused. He needed Katie with him. That way, he knew she was safe.

If anything happened to her and he was not there, he would never have been able to forgive himself. He couldn't go through that again. It had taken him a long time to shake the guilt and pain over the loss of his wife. When she died, he swore he would never go back undercover again, but he saw no other way. He was going to find out what kind of man Carlos Zambeni was, then he would see Crystal.

The plane landed at Stanfield International Airport. Michael got their bags, and they drove out of the city. The noise and traffic dissipated as he and Katie sped towards Nova Scotia's South Shore. Michael's spirits even started to improve as they neared the farm. CSIS had moved his mother here for protection following the explosion.

He slowed the car and pulled in a driveway lined on either side by old, gnarled maple trees. The house was white clapboard. It was one of those classic colonial homes the area was renowned for. It had a feeling of mellowness about it that captured your attention.

Some of the windowpanes were antique, hand-painted, stained glass dating back to the previous century, and there was a working fireplace in every room. The house had been built in the late eighteen hundreds. The property was dotted with barns and small cottages that housed the field hands needed to maintain the massive fields, gardens, and grounds.

His mother swung open the back screen door as he climbed out of the car. She ran up to him and threw her arms around his neck. "Michael, it's so good to see you. Where's Katie?" she asked, searching the car.

"She's asleep in the back. She's tired out. I'm going to carry her upstairs and tuck her in."

He lifted Katie's limp little body from the backseat. She moaned, and her eyelids fluttered slightly. He carried her up the winding staircase and nudged open the door to her room. It was decorated in pink and white. There was a stately brass four-post bed with a canopy against one wall. Pale-pink curtains hung around the window seat that overlooked the extensive gardens in the back. As he tucked her under the thick, flowered, homemade quilt, Katie rolled towards the center of the bed, and her breathing returned to a steady rhythm.

Michael went back downstairs and found his mother sitting on the chesterfield in the living room. He looked around, enjoying the familiar feeling of the room that surrounded him. The room was decorated in early twentieth century antiques that were a love of his mother.

Michael looked at her as he poured her wine. She was a beautiful woman for her seventy-five years. If you didn't know how old she was, you'd swear she was ten years younger. Her long gray hair was tied back in a ponytail, and the pale-yellow man's cotton shirt she wore hung loosely over faded blue jeans. She wore Birkenstock sandals, and the right one dangled from her foot. Her hazel eyes showed a wealth of wisdom behind their sparkle, indicating she knew more than what you were telling her.

"What's wrong, Michael? There's something really bothering you. I've not seen you like this since Katrina died. Have there been threats made against Katie?" she asked cautiously.

Michael looked at her. "No Mom. It's a long story."

"I have all night. We best get started. I want to know what you're getting yourself into," she said, tucking her legs underneath her body and making herself comfortable.

Michael relaxed in the La-Z-Boy opposite his mother. He had known when he arrived that he would have to tell

105

her everything. His only concern was telling her in a way that she wouldn't worry about him while he was gone.

"I've met someone. Her name is Crystal," Michael began.

"That's wonderful, Michael! What does she think of Katie?" Virginia's eyebrows raised as she gazed at her son. "As far as Katie is concerned, there's no problem. Crystal loves Katie, and Katie loves her."

"What's the trouble? There's more to this than a simple relationship, isn't there?"

"Yes," Michael replied, shifting his position in the chair.

Michael repeated the story of meeting Crystal, finding out she was a missing child, locating her parents, and her leaving for Calgary and getting a job with Carlos Zambeni. He told her Crystal had decided to stay in Alberta and not return to Newfoundland.

"I'm going there to try to convince her to come back. I'm following my instincts – they've never let me down before. There was only one time I didn't act on them. My instincts were right but I just didn't listen."

"You have concerns about this man, Carlos?"

"Yes, I do. A lot doesn't make sense in the story. I'm going to see Ed Billings at CSIS and have him run an in-depth check on Zambeni and his business. Then I'm going to fly to Calgary and see what else I can find out before I see Crystal. She'll never believe me without proof. When I see her, I want all the proof I can uncover."

"Do you think Carlos could be dangerous?" Virginia looked concerned.

Her son was always careful. She never worried about that, but he was continually getting himself into scrapes that were extremely dangerous. He was like a magnet for danger; it followed him everywhere. She remembered her feelings when he joined CSIS. She knew it would be dangerous, but he'd always dreamed of working undercover for the government.

She had taught him to relentlessly pursue his dreams. He had been a special agent investigating organized crime. He'd worked in Vancouver, Montreal, and Winnipeg, and his love for his job had cost him his wife and his partner. Following the explosion, he swore he would never go back. Now, he was telling her he was getting involved in undercover work again for a woman.

"Michael, have you heard from Dreamweaver?" Virginia hated to bring it up. Dreamweaver was suspected of having been behind the explosion that had ripped through his home. Michael had sent his partner, Brian, to get Katrina, and he had also been killed. Katie had been with her that weekend. Michael blamed himself for their deaths.

"No, not a word. I don't know what happened to him. It seems that after the accident he disappeared. I've watched the circuits, but there hasn't been anything. I'm going to ask Ed if they've come across him."

"Have you mentioned any of this to Crystal? Does she know about your background? What happened? What you did for a living?"

"No, I told her my wife died in an accident. I'll tell her if it works out. There's no reason to reveal the truth yet."

"When are you leaving?"

"Friday. Ed is going to meet me at the airport. From there, I'll fly to Calgary. That's why I want to leave Katie with you. I'm not sure how long this is going to take. Plus, I don't know what I might come up against. I know Katie will be safe here with you."

The grandfather clock in the hallway struck two, and its gongs echoed throughout the house. Michael stood up and placed his empty glass on the bar. "I'm going to call it a night. I'm exhausted. I don't think there's going to be any danger in this, and I don't want you to worry. I've told Katie I'm going to see Crystal and try to convince her to come home, that's all. She's growing up and notices things so easily. I must be careful with what she hears."

"Have you told her the truth about her mother?" Virginia asked as she stood up and snuffed out the candles burning along the mantel.

"No, I'm not going to tell her until she's old enough to understand the story properly. Telling her now would only scare her."

"Yes, you're probably right. It'll be great to have her here with me while you're gone. Since your father died, it's been lonely. Good night, Michael. Sleep well," Virginia said, as she made her way up the stairs to her bedroom.

"Good night, Mom," Michael replied, climbing the stairs behind her to the second floor.

Over the next couple of days, Michael tried to concentrate on Katie. They went on picnics, went horseback riding and took long walks through the forest that surrounded the house. On the day Michael planned to leave, he and Katie walked through the pine grove behind the house to the duck pond. The boughs rustled in the breeze, and a flock of Canada geese on their yearly migration landed like a blanket to cover the pond.

"They're wonderful, aren't they?" Katie said, looking up at her father.

"Yes, they are, sweetheart," Michael replied, watching her eyes shine with delight.

"Are you going to be gone for a long time, Dad?" she asked, as sadness clouded the brilliance on her face.

"I hope not. I hope it won't take too long to convince Crystal to come back. You'd be happy if I brought her back, wouldn't you?" Michael asked, squatting down beside her.

"Oh yes! I love Crystal. Will you bring her back here?" Katie exclaimed, the brightness returning to her eyes.

"Yes, we'll get you first thing, I promise. You can show her Midnight, and we can both introduce her to your grandmother. How would that be?"

"That would be awesome! I can't wait to see her," Katie exclaimed.

"One thing, Katie. Once I leave, I won't be able to call you very much. I'll call as often as I can."

Katie looked intently at her father. "That's okay. I'll take care of Gramma Virginia, and she'll take care of me. We'll be fine."

Michael looked at her and began to smile. Sometimes, she sounded and looked so much older than she was. She's really growing up, he thought.

Chapter 8

MICHAEL LOOKED OUT OF THE airplane window and stared into the darkness as the plane broke through the clouds over Ottawa. The city lights twinkled brightly in the dark. It had been three years since he was last in the city.

He left the plane, picked up his luggage, and proceeded to the arrival area of the airport where he knew Ed would be waiting. He walked through the automatic doors and could see Ed studying the arriving passengers. Their eyes met, and Ed started towards Michael, his hand extended in greeting.

"Hey, ol' pal. It sure is great to see you," he said, as their hands met in a tight handshake. "Let's get out of here. I hate the airport. You're out in the open far too much."

"You're always thinking like an agent. Don't you ever give it a rest?" Michael chuckled.

They loaded Michael's bags into the trunk of Ed's black sedan that was parked outside. Ed opened the passenger door for Michael, went around to the other side, and hopped behind the wheel.

"I thought we'd take a trip down memory lane and stop at Paddy's to talk. Okay with you?" Ed asked as he pulled out into traffic.

"Yeah, that's fine," Michael replied and glanced around at the familiar landmarks on the way.

Paddy's was a little pub where the CSIS agents spent their quiet time. There, they could sit and talk without being disturbed. Ed and Michael sat down and ordered a couple of draft beers. Ed told him how things had changed since he'd left. "The guys' morale has really dropped. Believe me, people are more careful with their families since Katrina and Brian. Brian's death hit us all hard. He was a good man. When you decided to leave, it was downhill from there," Ed said, taking a drink from his tumbler.

Ed began to study Michael. He looked good, a little tired, but that was normal. Michael worked too hard. He had always been the first one in the office in the morning, and the last one to leave at night if he left at all. He was a true bloodhound when it came to tracking someone. Michael was after someone. Ed could see it.

"Who are you after, Michael? Have you had any intel on Dreamweaver?"

"No, nothing. But now that you mention him, has there been anything on him since the explosion?" Michael's voice was low and controlled.

"Nothing! I've tried to keep up on him. It seems like he dropped off the face of the earth. I've talked to Randy and Bill about it. They haven't seen anything on him either. We figure he changed his name and is laying low. I don't think the people he worked for were too impressed with the job. That bomb was meant to take you out. Since then, you've dropped out of sight, too. He's waiting for you to resurface. Have you been keeping an eye out for him?"

"Yes, I have. Having him find me in a small town in Newfoundland might not be easy as I don't think it's a place he would look. I had to start over in a place where I was invisible. Things are quiet, and it's a pleasant change. I'm in charge of the missing children and runaway division."

"You're chasing a missing kid? That's what brings you back to the Hill?" Ed's eyebrows rose in surprise.

"Not exactly, but it's how I became involved and how this all started."

Michael told Ed about Crystal and his feelings for her. Ed listened closely as Michael began to describe Carlos Zambeni and his suspicions.

"I don't know who this guy is and what he wants with Crystal, but it sounds suspicious to me. No one hires an untrained assistant to help scout fashion models. They hire someone experienced who knows what they're doing. I came to Ottawa to see if you'd help me do a little digging into Mr. Zambeni and his company before I investigate him in Alberta."

"Are you sure you're not acting on your emotions, Michael?" Ed asked in a concerned voice. "She's a grown woman. You may not want to hear this, old pal, but maybe she wasn't as into you as you thought she was. Once she got to Calgary, she realized you were just another guy. Some women are like that, you know."

"I know what you're thinking, Ed, but Crystal isn't like that. She loves me – I know she does. She's been overwhelmed by the wealth and power of her family and having someone like Carlos interested in her. You know men like him. They only have their own interests in mind. Girls like Crystal are easy prey. She's going to get hurt. I'm going to try to prevent that. I love her, Ed."

"I can see that, Michael. I just hope you're not letting your emotions cloud your judgement."

"Let's not argue, buddy. I know what I'm doing. I need your help to get into the CSIS files. We can run a check on Carlos and his company from there."

"We can go into the office first thing in the morning and get started. What happens if you don't come up with anything incriminating? What then?"

"I'll have to win her back the old-fashioned way, with charm!" Michael laughed.

Ed dropped Michael off at his hotel and promised to return in the morning. Michael picked up the key to his room and stepped into the elevator. One thing Ed had said began to bother him. What if he didn't find anything? What would he do then? What if Crystal didn't feel the same way about him? Michael drove these thoughts from his mind. No, Crystal loved him; her eyes told him that. He was sure there was something to find on Carlos, and no matter how long it took him, he would find it.

Michael was up, dressed, and downstairs waiting for Ed when he pulled up in front of the hotel the next morning.

"What took you so long? I've been waiting forever," Michael said, ribbing his friend.

"I'm not like you. I can't function without sleep." Ed laughed.

Michael felt the knot in his stomach tightening as they walked up the front steps of CSIS headquarters. He tried to shake the feeling beginning to descend on him.

"You all right? You look kind of pale," Ed asked, looking at him.

"Yeah, I'll be fine," Michael replied, pulling open the front door and stepping into the lobby.

Michael glanced out the window behind Ed's desk at the Parliament Buildings.

"You have an awesome view," Michael remarked, nodding towards the Parliament Buildings.

"I hardly notice until someone mentions it. Let's get started," he replied, sitting down at his computer.

Michael stood directly behind Ed, who began feeding the computer information. He pressed enter and the computer began a search.

"It's going to take a while. Why don't we get a cup of coffee and come back? I know the guys would love to see you," Ed said, walking towards the door.

Michael followed reluctantly. The last thing he wanted was to reminisce with the guys. He wanted to forget about everything here. Ed had agreed to help him, though, and he didn't want to appear ungrateful, so he followed him down the familiar hallway that would lead past his old office door.

"Randy has taken over your office," Ed said, as they passed the open door. Michael glanced in and nodded at Randy, who was studying an array of open files on his desk.

They entered the empty coffee room and poured

themselves a cup. Randy was in the doorway as they prepared to leave. "I thought that was you, Michael. Are you coming back to work? We could sure use you," he said, smiling and extending his hand.

Michael shook his hand. "Not at all. I thought I'd drop in to say hello while I'm in the city."

Michael passed by Randy hurriedly and returned to Ed's office, anxious to escape the questions he saw in Randy's eyes. He didn't want to get involved in any conversations about the past, present or future, nor did he want to have to explain what he was doing in Ottawa. He wanted the information on Zambeni and to get on a plane for Alberta.

The computer finished spitting out the requested information as Michael and Ed entered the office. Ed ripped off the sheets, glanced briefly at them and passed them on to Michael. Michael reviewed them and glanced up. "I told you there was something strange about this man," he said, with a hint of excitement in his voice.

"Don't start getting excited, Michael. There's really nothing out of the ordinary except a few minor offences," Ed replied.

"Minor, yes, but the information on the company and the people he seems to be connected with are very intriguing indeed. His business dealings take him to interesting parts of the United States and around the world, on what looks to be a regular schedule, don't you think?"

Michael reviewed the description of Carlos again: five feet ten inches tall, dark complexion, slightly wavy dark hair, dark eyes, one hundred and ninety pounds. His date of birth was November 2, 1980, and he had been born in Milan, Italy. His mother had been born in Bogota, Columbia, and his father had been born in Milan. He had immigrated to Canada in 1998.

"Ed, look at this. He's worked in New York, Miami, Vancouver, Winnipeg, and Montreal before moving to Calgary. He was a shipping/receiving clerk for some of the shadiest companies these cities have to offer. He's been picked up for small-time trafficking but has never done any time for any of the charges. The thing that surprises me is that after the fourth offence in Montreal, he moved to Calgary and started this company. Do you want to explain to me where a two-bit hood like Carlos gets the capital and backing to begin a business in a field he knows nothing about? Also, his company profits and reputation have flourished in the influential circles of the Calgary business community. Either he has some pretty big names behind him, or he's one incredibly good con-artist."

Ed watched Michael. He saw the familiar gleam in his eyes as he read the sheets of information. He hoped this would bring Michael back to Ottawa and thought that, once this was over, Michael would realize how much he missed being an agent.

"I agree. There seems to be a lot of questions floating around in the background of Carlos Zambeni. I know one thing: you have to take this one slow and be careful about what accusations you make. Carlos has friends in high places."

Ed started typing on the computer, and seconds later a photograph of Carlos appeared on the screen, along with a driver's license number, current address and the makes and models of the vehicles registered to him. Ed printed the information and passed it to Michael, "This is all we have on him, and you certainly didn't get the information from me. The director would have my head if he knew I was handing personal information on people over to you. Even if you were one of the best agents we ever had."

"I know, Ed, and thanks. I hope I can put this information to good use before Crystal gets in trouble, is hurt or worse," Michael said, putting all the sheets of paper in an envelope. He stood up and shook Ed's hand. "I'm going to Calgary to start digging right away."

Michael tucked the envelope into the inside pocket of his jacket. Ed stood up and walked around the desk. "I'll walk you out. It's been good seeing you. If you decide you want to come back, let me know, and I'll speak to the brass. I'm sure they'd want you back as much as we all do."

"Thanks, Ed. I want to find Carlos, get Crystal, and be on my way home."

Ed and Michael walked out the front doors of the building and stood on the sidewalk. "If there's anything else you need, let me know. If things start to get carried away, call me. I'll come out and give you a hand. The two of us working together again would be great."

Michael looked at his friend. Ed was one of a kind. "Thanks again. I promise to keep in touch."

Ed watched Michael climb into a waiting cab and waved one last time as the car pulled out onto the street and disappeared among the morning traffic.

Michael landed in Calgary, retrieved his luggage, and walked to the Hertz counter to rent a vehicle. He checked into his hotel, went to the dining room to eat, and then went to the Calgary Police headquarters. Michael entered the building and was met at the counter by a young red-haired girl with deep emerald eyes.

"I'd like to see your chief of police," he said, pulling his badge from his pocket.

"Just a second," she replied, glancing at him with curiosity.

She returned with a tall, heavy-set man in his mid-fifties. He had dark, friendly eyes, and his gray hair was thinning on top. He extended a hand. "Welcome to Calgary, Blackburn. We've been expecting you. I'm Joe Parker."

Michael looked at him, surprised. "Thanks, Chief, but I don't understand."

"Ed Billings called me this morning. We go way back. He told me you were on your way, and even though you're no longer with CSIS we are to help you out all we can. So, whatever you need, just ask. Come to my office, and you can fill me in on what you're going to be doing here in the city."

"Ed's a great guy," Michael said, sitting down.

Joe made notes as Michael told his story and explained why he was in Calgary and what he would be doing there.

"We've thought Zambeni was up to something. He's slippery. We've never been able to get anything concrete on him. He runs a so-called modeling agency and travels a great deal. His trips are mostly continental, but there are times when he travels abroad. His history is one of a small-town hood. Who it is, we don't know. Things with Zambeni are clean, at least as far as we can tell. We haven't been able to pin anything on him."

"What do you know about the Pearson Computers and

Electronics Corporation?" Michael asked.

"Let's see. It's a privately owned company and run by Amanda Pearson. She's not the CEO – her husband Jonathan is. There's a son, Allen, who we've wondered about. He doesn't seem to be the boardroom type. He spends time with pretty shady characters but has never been in any trouble. He's the spoiled brat playboy type. Nothing threatening."

"Has there ever been any connection between the Zambeni outfit and Pearson Computers?" Michael asked.

"Pearson Computers does hold the smaller contracts for security and computer software technology for the Zambeni outfit, but nothing major. There have been rumours Allen is trying hard to get exclusive contracts with them, but nothing has materialized that I'm aware of. Carlos is someone you really don't want to cross, so I've assigned you a partner while you're here. Just as a precaution."

Joe buzzed his intercom, and his office door opened. Michael turned around and saw a man in his mid-thirties, of medium height with a stocky build enter the room. His hair was cropped short, and it had a strawberry blond hue. His blue eyes held questions as to who Michael might be. He was dressed in a t-shirt and jeans and looked more like a university student than a police officer.

"Trevor Banks, Michael Blackburn," Joe said, introducing them.

Michael stood, shook his hand, and turned towards Joe. "You know, this isn't necessary. I'm quite capable of taking care of myself."

"Nonsense, Blackburn. Trevor knows the city and has

contacts in places you'll need. His experience will be invaluable to you. Right now, you could use someone to show you around and how things work here. Trevor is the best undercover cop we have. No one knows his connections to this department. He's been underground for four years now."

"I can see your point, but right now there's just me. If I disappear, then so be it. I don't want to have to worry about someone else," Michael said reluctantly.

"Ed filled me in on your history. I'm sorry to hear about what happened. I can understand what you're saying. No one knows you're here, and no one knows Trevor is connected to this department. He could get you into places you'd never be able to go without suspicion.

You won't threaten his cover because no one in this city knows who you are. As far as Trevor goes, you're a long-lost cousin who moved to the city to find investors and drum up business. I don't want you going out on the streets digging into the backgrounds of people without any backup. I don't want to be responsible for you turning up on a slab at the morgue. Get my drift?"

Michael turned towards the door. "Well, since he's going to be tagging along with me, let's get going. Time's a-wasting. I want to do research before I hit the streets."

Trevor stepped forward and opened the file he had been holding under his arm.

"Joe told me what you were looking into, so I took the liberty of doing some preliminary work before you arrived. I've compiled a list of Carlos's business associates, employees, and travel schedule, and I've put together a portfolio on his social contacts and who he spends his time with.

There's a new girl in his life, one Crystal Pearson. She's the long-lost daughter of Jonathan and Amanda Pearson, the owners of Pearson Computers. She was kidnapped years ago, and as it turns out is back with her family. She's his new toy and is traveling abroad with him now. He hired her to work for him. It's puzzling, really, as she has no experience in the position she's been hired for."

"I know all about her. She's the reason I'm here," Michael said shortly.

"You and Crystal have a history?" Trevor exclaimed, studying Michael's face.

"Yes, we do," Michael snapped, letting him know he was not prepared to go into further detail. "When she told me she was taking a job with Carlos, that sparked my curiosity, too. What would Carlos want with someone who has no experience? That led me to believe something was up. I decided to come west and check it out."

"You guys go to Trevor's office and continue this conversation," Joe interrupted. "I've got work to do. Now that you're in Trevor's capable hands, I feel much better. If you can help us nail this Carlos guy, then great! It would be one more slime ball off the streets."

Trevor led Michael towards his office. "My office is at your disposal. I'll introduce you as a visiting cousin of mine from back east who's come to Calgary looking for investors and to do business.

My identity is solid in the underground. I've never been linked to any of the arrests and have kept my pseudonym well guarded. As far as you're concerned, my name is Terry Hill, and under no circumstances will you call me anything else and blow my cover. My life and safety depend on it. If you research me on the law enforcement computers, my rap sheet is as long as your arm. I'm well respected in the circles I travel."

Michael knew how dangerous it was and what the consequences could be if Trevor's true identity was revealed. Michael had worked undercover in some of the meanest, hardest parts of the bigger Canadian cities and decided he'd better prepare himself for a trip down memory lane. It was one trip he didn't want to take, but if Crystal was getting herself into trouble and needed his help, he felt he had no choice.

Michael and Trevor worked at the office most of the day. Trevor explained as much of the workings of Zambeni's business as he could, and Michael pulled information on the Pearsons and their company.

Trevor broke Michael's concentration. "Hey, do you ever stop to eat or anything?"

Michael looked up and smiled. "Yeah, once in a while."

"Listen, why don't you call it a day? Go back to your hotel, get some rest and something to eat, then meet me downtown. I'll start introducing you to people," Trevor suggested.

"Sounds good. The lines are beginning to blend together," Michael replied, rubbing his eyes.

"I'll meet you at Club 2440 at seven-thirty. Don't be late. Timing is everything there," Trevor said as he turned and walked out a back door of the station into the alley. Michael followed him out the door and watched him pull away in a candy-apple red 1965 Thunderbird. Nice car, Michael thought to himself.

Michael arrived at his hotel, showered, and changed into a light gray silk shirt and jeans. He took his long, dark-haired wig from its box, slicked it back with gel, tied it into a tight ponytail and placed it securely to his head. He added his gold wire-rimmed glasses, put gold chains around his neck and placed a two-karat diamond stud in his earlobe. He looked in the mirror and was pleased at how his beard had grown almost a full two inches since he'd left Newfoundland. He slipped on a navy-blue sports coat, looked at himself in the mirror and was satisfied with his appearance.

He stopped at the front desk in the lobby to deposit his badge in the hotel safe and stepped through the revolving doors onto the street. His insides began to knot, and his skin began to tingle. The old feeling was coming back. He used to love the adrenaline rush undercover work gave him, but not anymore. Michael hailed a cab and gave the driver the address. He looked at Michael carefully and sped off towards his passenger's requested destination.

2440 was a high-profile nightclub, and Michael decided when he stepped out of the cab and onto the street that he would keep an extremely low profile. The music could be heard clearly as he sauntered towards the door, where he was greeted by a big burly young man dressed in a muscle shirt revealing at least fifteen-inch biceps. Great! Here I go again, Michael thought, as he pulled open the door and stepped across the threshold into the darkness of the club.

The music hit Michael like a wall when he stepped inside. He stopped to let his eyes adjust to the flashing lights and darkness. The crowd was a mixture of middle and upper-class, professionals, and entertainers. Michael took notice of a few celebrities mulling about the bar. Girls in short shorts and halter tops weaved through and around the crowd serving drinks. Dancers on a stage in the middle of the floor swung aimlessly around poles, looking bored.

Tables and chairs were strategically positioned throughout the club, and large plush booths surrounded the outside walls. The bar was Honduran mahogany and was encircled with a highly polished brass rail. Glasses hung upside down above the bar, and the bartenders were pouring and mixing drinks as if in a well-rehearsed dance number.

Michael ordered a rye and Coke and surveyed the room around him. It didn't take him long to spot Trevor in one of the extra-large booths with his friends. Michael strolled up to the booth and looked directly at him. "I was told I'd find you here, Terry. How ya been?"

Terry smiled, stood up and extended his hand. "Michael! I heard you were coming to town. Good to see you. It's been a while."

Terry looked to his left and nodded to the man sitting in a black Armani suit. "This is Michael Hamilton, a cousin of mine from back east. You and he might have mutual business interests."

"Is that so? Come sit down," Donavan said in a low baritone.

Michael slid into the booth across from Donavan and studied the man. He looked to be about forty-five years old. He had a rugged face and beady dark eyes. His beard was short and neatly trimmed against his prominent jawline. His black hair was thin, and silver threads peeked sporadically throughout. He looked to be a fit two hundred pounds, and his voice was low and deep.

"Terry tells me you're extensively involved in real estate. I thought I'd take a trip out here to try to drum up parties interested in helping to redevelop abandoned towns and neighbourhoods. Since the economic downturn, there are a lot of houses that are vacant and can be bought up cheap. The right investors with a solid business plan could stand to make an excellent return on their money. I'd like to sit down with you and go over my plan for re-establishing these neighbourhoods."

Donavan looked at Michael and smiled. "This is the first time I've ever had someone from back east try to sell me real estate in the west. I'm aware of the dilapidated neighbour-hoods and towns across the country. I've been studying the market quite carefully. It's a matter of trying to decide where the best place to invest is for the best possible results."

Michael nodded in agreement. "I can understand that. I'd like the opportunity to show you what myself and others have been looking at in Alberta and Saskatchewan. Once you've had the chance to go over the proposal and listen to what I have to offer, I think you'll find it would be the best place to put your money."

"Call my office and set up an appointment to come in. I'll at least listen to what you have to say," Donavan replied.

Michael stood up to go. "Until then."

"It was good seeing you, Michael," Terry said, turning around and sitting back down.

Michael pushed his way through the crowd to the exit, anxious to get outside onto the sidewalk and into the night air. As he reached the exit, he noticed a young man in his late twenties who was drinking heavily. He was staggering along the side of the bar, trying to find a seat. Michael walked over and took the young man by the arm to help him sit down.

"Hey, thanks!" the young man slurred.

"No problem, buddy. I noticed you were having a little trouble."

"Yeah, a bit too much tonight. The guy at the bar is calling my limo. Can I give you a ride? My name is Allen Pearson."

The limo driver arrived and stepped up to the two men. "Mr. Pearson, I'm parked right outside the door. Let me help you," he said, taking Allen by the arm.

Michael followed Allen into the back of the limo as the driver shut the door. "Can you drop me at the Palliser first?" Michael requested.

Allen was dressed in a light-green polo shirt and dark trousers. Michael had seen his kind before. Overly rich, bored young men who couldn't walk away from the family money to strike out on their own. Allen was handsome, rich, and fun-loving from what Michael could tell. He was stuck in the game and couldn't get out.

"So, what do you do, Allen?" Michael asked, starting the conversation.

"I run part of Pearson Computers. My mother and father are the owners and founders. I work for them." "What about family? Do you have a wife, children, brothers, or sisters?" Michael continued.

"Yeah, I have a sister. My long-lost sister," he said sarcastically. "She was kidnapped, and we've just found her after twenty years. She was working for us, then she met Carlos Zambeni, and now she works for him. Just like that! She has no experience that would benefit him. I'm not sure why she left our company. But she's gone. They're traveling in Europe."

Allen rambled on. "Crystal, that's my sister, is a beautiful girl, so I can see Carlos taking right to her. I don't understand why he wants to use my sister to work for him. He's a dirt bag, and I don't like him one little bit. He's one of those guys you're always wondering about, you know what I mean?"

Michael listened carefully. This was Crystal's brother, and if he didn't know what Carlos wanted with Crystal it might be harder to find out what he was up to than Michael thought.

Michael chuckled to himself when he reviewed the events of the evening. He had impressed Donavan, but he didn't expect to run into Crystal's brother Allen on the same night. Maybe his luck in the field was changing. Michael could see through the window that they were getting close to his hotel. "Listen, Allen, give me your phone number. I'll give you a call this week, and we'll have lunch. I'd like to pay you back for the ride."

"Sure, that sounds great. Give me a call, and we'll set something up," Allen said, scribbling his number on the back of a match package from the bar.

Michael took the number and hopped out. "Talk to you later this week, Allen. Thanks for the ride." And he closed the limo door.

Michael took a short walk around the block to clear his

head and review the events of the day. He had been invited to set up a meeting with Donavan and had accidently run into Allen, Crystal's brother. He would try his best to become his friend. He would have to do his research before he set up the lunch. Michael pulled the large glass door to the hotel open and stepped inside. Yes, he thought. It has been a particularly good night.

Chapter 9

CRYSTAL CRAWLED OUT OF BED in the early morning, feeling the after-effects of the champagne from the night before, and still feeling a sense of emptiness. What was wrong with her? Carlos was a perfect gentleman. He had given her an amazing opportunity. She didn't want to blow it over her not feeling up to being his partner on the trip. She could learn from him, and he was showing her things she had never seen before. What difference did it make that there didn't seem to be the same feeling for him as she had for Michael? She had to get over Michael and experience a different type of lifestyle.

She called Ava's room, and the woman who answered the telephone replied, "I'm sorry, Miss, but she's out. I expect her back shortly. I'll have her contact your room when she returns."

Crystal called Carlos. "Carlos Zambeni," his voice

boomed into the receiver.

"Hi, Carlos, it's Crystal. What time do you want to get started this morning?"

"I'm waiting for Ava to return from her meeting. She shouldn't be much longer getting back. I'll let you know," he said, hanging up the phone.

Crystal looked around the room and noticed a silver coffee service sitting on a trolley tucked behind the door against the wall. She went over and poured herself a cup and looked into the closet to try to figure out what to wear. She pulled a clean pair of jeans off a hanger, decided on a plain white t-shirt, and laced up her Nikes.

Crystal entered the dining room of the hotel and scanned the room for a table. The room was filled with businesspeople, tourists, and locals. She walked over, sat down, and picked up the menu laying in front of her. A waitress approached her with a coffee pot in hand. "Coffee, Miss?" she asked, waving the pot towards the cup.

"Yes, please," Crystal replied, without looking up.

"The garden omelette is really good here, if you're having a tough time making up your mind," the waitress suggested as she poured the coffee.

"That sounds good," Crystal said, passing her the menu.

As Crystal waited for her breakfast to arrive, she glanced around. The room was ballroom-like with large crystal chandeliers hanging overhead. There were staircases running up both sides of the room to a dining loft overlooking the room below.

The tables were draped in white linen tablecloths and set with polished silver utensils. Crystal glanced out into the foyer. Carlos and Ava stood together having a heated discussion. As they looked towards her, their facial expressions changed to smiles of greeting. They walked into the dining room and up to the table intending to join her.

"There you are, Crystal! We thought you might have wandered off on your own. If you're going somewhere, please let us know. We don't want to lose you," Carlos said immediately.

Carlos looked at the way she was dressed and was clearly upset. "We're working today, Crystal. I expect you to dress like it."

"I wasn't sure whether you wanted me to stand out or not. I thought we were observing today, so I wanted to be comfortable," she replied.

"We'll be looking at potential models today, but there are a lot of places you may not be able to enter dressed like that."

"I was thinking, Carlos, if we're looking for fresh faces, why not look in new places and try new ideas? What about a fresh country look for a change? Something natural. There's so much emphasis put on overly thin, upscale, and expensive looks. Why not bring in a line of fresh, new, everyday faces to attract all types of women to the products you're selling?"

Carlos looked at Ava, and she returned his gaze. "What an idea! Why don't we take a drive out into the countryside and visit the small towns and villages instead of sitting around stuffy restaurants and wandering through shopping malls?"

Carlos called for the Rolls, and it wasn't long before they were speeding through London. He seemed happy with her new idea of incorporating the modern, everyday-looking woman into the mix. As they drove past the greenery of the English countryside, Carlos and Ava sifted through piles of pictures of different women and men. Models sent their pictures into the company for consideration hoping something about them would attract the scouts.

"This one would look good in the ad for the new night-club opening this fall. She might also do for the computer ad we want to run online," Ava said, placing the young woman's photograph to the side.

"Crystal, I want you to look through this pile of pictures and tell me who might attract you to visit a nightclub," Carlos said, handing her a pile of photographs.

Crystal started flipping through the pictures. By the time the car had stopped outside a small pub in the village of Carlisle, the women were beginning to all look alike. There was nothing natural about the pictures. It was hard to distinguish one woman from another.

The day turned into driving around and visiting pubs, restaurants, shops, and small parks in every town and village they could find. They spent time talking to women and men, getting to know them and their backgrounds and if they might be interested in pursuing a career in modeling. Out of all the candidates, only three were interested in traveling into London for a photo-shoot.

Carlos agreed on one girl Crystal had picked out and the other two Ava had chosen. She had seen things in a couple of the girls Crystal hadn't noticed. When they arrived back at the hotel, Crystal excused herself and went to her room to shower and change. They were supposed to be going out.

She wanted to ready herself for a night on the town. Carlos disappeared into his room, saying that he had phone calls to make and emails to look after. He would meet her in the lobby at eight.

Crystal wasn't sure where Ava had gone. She wouldn't be joining them on their evening out. "Ava doesn't go out once our work day is finished. She prefers to stay in her room and continue working or relaxing in the tub. She leaves the nightlife part of the business to me," Carlos informed her.

"I'm thinking of doing the same thing tonight, Carlos, if you don't mind. It's been a long day for me. The time change is still affecting me."

"Very well, Crystal. Don't make a habit of cooping yourself up in the evenings. I like my partners to be at my side when I'm out in the evenings."

"I'm tired, Carlos. I need rest. I'll be more myself in the morning."

Over the next couple of weeks, they travelled to Paris, Berlin, and Rome. There were outings to museums, historic sites, and social events every evening. Crystal was exhausted from the parties and was already looking forward to getting back to Calgary. The nightlife of the big cities was not what she had imagined.

Ava made herself scarce during the trip, and Carlos seemed to be wrapped up in business affairs. Crystal was beginning to wonder exactly why she was on the trip and what her purpose was. As far as she could tell, she didn't have a job. It seemed her job was to be the new girl Carlos was dating.

Carlos arranged for her to have people do her makeup

and dress her. He was overly concerned about her outward appearance, and she was getting annoyed with the constant fussing. She wasn't used to being pampered and living a life of leisure. She liked to be out doing things and meeting people. She began to wonder if she had made the right decision by leaving the family business and going to work for Carlos. He seemed more interested in having people look at his new girlfriend than being interested in what she could do. He was more than supportive with her current ideas, and some of them seemed to be working out well. The natural women ads were taking off, and the client was thrilled with the results they were generating. Carlos was happy, too. The more ads he sold, the more money he made.

Crystal often wondered what Carlos did during the day. He and Ava would lock themselves up in his hotel room going over paperwork that she was not privy to. Their meetings were private, and when they were through, there was never any discussion about what was being planned.

Ava had concerns about customs and was having a problem with one of the girls traveling back to Calgary. Carlos didn't seem bothered by the little hiccup and tried to reassure Ava all would be well. He told her he would make a few phone calls to straighten out the paperwork needed for the young woman to enter Canada. Crystal was beginning to feel more like an ornament than an employee. She stood and stared out at the streets of Rome and thought, I wonder what Michael is doing? I miss Corner Brook.

Crystal received an email from Gloria about Samuel, and it triggered her to think about the simple way of life she once knew. It seemed so long ago that she was sitting at Gloria's kitchen table, drinking coffee, and watching the kids play in the backyard.

She talked to Carlos about children. He was dead set against them. He didn't have time, nor did he want whining brats bothering him after a long day at work. He wasn't interested in procreating at all. This saddened Crystal as she was looking forward to being a mother some day.

There were many differences between them, and the more time Crystal spent with Carlos, the more she realized how different they were. They had different priorities and different ways of looking at things. She still felt an emptiness inside whenever they were together intimately. There was something missing and something quite different about Carlos.

The private jet landed at the airport in Calgary without even a bump. The flight had been so smooth that Crystal hardly knew she was in the air. She'd spent the flight reading and catching up on the news from home.

Amanda had sent her an email to inform her that Allen was continuing to look for another assistant to help him. He liked Sandra as his secretary, and he didn't want to replace her. She was particularly good at her job and kept him organized.

Allen had made a new contact one night and seemed to be spending his time doing business with him. He was into real estate development and was in Calgary to look for property and investors. Amanda had few details about the contact, but she was encouraged that the time Allen was spending would pay off big eventually.

The Pearson limousine was there to pick her up at the

airport, and Crystal sank into the seat and laid her head back, closing her eyes. She was happy to be back. She missed the craziness of the family: Allen's constant ribbing, Maria's continuous smile, her father's passive nature, and even her mother's continual bickering and complaining.

Crystal thought about calling Michael but decided against it. He'd made it clear during their last conversation that he wasn't interested in continuing a relationship with her if she was involved with Carlos. But was she even involved with Carlos? She had no idea whether she was an ornament on his arm, a valued employee, or another diversion.

She missed Michael and wondered how Katie was. *I guess it wouldn't be such a smart idea to call. It could upset Katie,* Crystal thought. She decided to call Gloria when she arrived home. Gloria would know how Michael and Katie were doing. It would be good to talk to someone she was close to.

The limo pulled up outside the entrance to the Pearson property. Crystal still found it hard to believe she lived in a house surrounded by an iron fence, a gate and security cameras. She had everything she had ever wanted at her fingertips. She had spent so many lean years with Samuel moving from place to place and living in dumps and dives. This was such a huge contrast to those cold nights in rooming houses and dirty motel housekeeping rooms.

Maria came to the door to meet her, followed by a tall young man who took her luggage. "Welcome home, Miss. We've missed you. This is Jacob. He's new and oversees the gardening, pool, and anything else we can find for him to do. He'll take your luggage to your room. Mr. and Mrs.

Pearson will be down shortly, and Allen should be home momentarily. They've been anxiously awaiting your arrival. Everyone has missed you and is excited to hear about your trip."

Amanda was coming down the stairs as Crystal entered the foyer. "Welcome home, Crystal. It's good to see you. Did you have a good trip?"

Crystal nodded. "Yes, I did. I'm anxious to freshen up before dinner if there's enough time."

"Take all the time you need, dear. Dinner will wait until you're ready. Allen isn't home yet, and your father just came in from the greenhouse. He'll be a while getting ready. We're looking forward to hearing the stories of your travels."

"I shouldn't be more than an hour," Crystal replied, climbing the staircase towards her bedroom. She was looking forward to a hot bath and some peace and quiet. She opened the door to her room and noticed her luggage had already been emptied and put away.

She opened the closet door and pulled out her old, faded, green terrycloth bathrobe. It was her favourite, and she liked the way it made her feel when she put it on. She pulled the collar up around her neck and gave herself a hug.

Maria had already run the water for her bath. She slipped beneath the bubbles into the hot liquid. It surrounded her, and she relished the heat against her skin. It sure beat struggling daily to make ends meet and wondering where your next meal was coming from. But there was something missing in her life, and she couldn't put her finger on it. She was sure it would come to her in time. For now, she was going to enjoy her bath and dinner with the family. It was good to be back.

When Crystal arrived in the dining room, everyone was seated. Allen was looking at her with curiosity in his eyes. She could tell by the look in Jonathan's eyes that he was genuinely happy to see her. Amanda was so fidgety that Crystal knew she was bursting with questions.

Amanda started the conversation. "Tell us how it went. What's your new job like with Carlos?"

Crystal hesitated, though there wasn't any reason not to tell them the whole story and how she was feeling.

"The new job is very confusing. I'm not sure what my job really is. I spent time on my own as Carlos and Ava met on a regular basis behind closed doors. I did come up with a few innovative ideas Carlos was satisfied with. One of them was the new natural woman ads his agency is running. He doesn't seem to have a lot for me to do.

We went to numerous social events where I nodded and said little. It's a strange world for me to be associated with. I'm not used to making small talk and socializing in those types of atmospheres. Big parties and galas were not something Samuel and I went to. I felt out of place most of the time. I did enjoy some of them though, and was able to meet a few nice people.

Ava, who is supposed to be my assistant, was always busy. If Carlos and I were out to an event, she stayed in her hotel room working. The models we hired should work out well. One had difficulty gaining entrance into Canada, but Carlos made a few phone calls and filled out extra paper-work, and she was allowed in. He didn't go into any details as to what the problem was, just that he had worked it out with the authorities.

Carlos and I spent time alone and did get along well. He's a nice man, but he's overly preoccupied with work and his business. He did make sure I was extremely comfortable and had everything I needed, though he wasn't around much during the day. He hired a driver to take me to all the sites I wanted to see, and I was able to shop wherever I wanted. I brought back a few trinkets for you. I hope you like them. I haven't known any of you long enough to know your specific tastes."

Dinner arrived and interrupted Crystal. Jonathan spoke up and commented on how happy he was that she'd had a good time, and he was happy to have her back safe. Allen sat quietly and listened to every detail of what she had to say.

"Why don't you come back to work for the company and leave Carlos to his globetrotting? It's not like you can't go anywhere you want while living with us. I could use the help. Roberta is a good assistant, but I'd much rather have you working by my side," Allen said, looking up from his dinner plate.

Crystal shot him a surprised glance. "I'll think about it. I didn't realize there would be so little for me to do in working for Carlos. I like to feel I'm contributing to something productive."

Allen changed the subject and began to talk about his new business acquaintance and how encouraged he was they were hitting it off.

"This guy is interesting, to say the least. He's in town for a few months. I'm not sure what he's into exactly. He has his fingers in a few pots. He's been working closely with

Donavan Whitman. That makes everyone sit up and take notice. Donavan is very picky about who he does business with.

I've been trying to get in to see Donavan for months. I haven't been able to set up a meeting. Donavan has extensive real estate holdings in and around the Calgary area and is mostly into nightclubs. He's highly successful and could use top-notch computer technicians and equipment to monitor the security systems in all his buildings.

Michael is someone I think you should meet, Crystal. He's about thirty and has no family. He's been alone for many years after a bad break-up right out of university. He has no one special in his life right now and doesn't seem interested in the many girls that have spent hours trying to get him to notice them."

"His name is Michael? I don't think so! I've had enough of men named Michael. I'm involved with Carlos, though I don't have any indication from him that we might be exclusive. I don't want to take the chance that he thinks we are and then upset him by meeting with someone else. If things with Carlos don't work out, I'm going to take a break from men for a while."

Allen laughed. "Carlos Zambeni doesn't tie himself down to one woman, Crystal. Everyone knows that! He's not in the modeling business for nothing. Carlos likes women. All kinds. He's not scared to show it. He spends a great deal of time among some of the world's most beautiful young women. You'll be another notch in his belt until someone else catches his eye. I'm sorry to sound so harsh, but Carlos is a very selfish man, and nothing comes between him, his business, and his women. Just a word of warning to you not to let yourself get too emotionally invested in a relationship with Carlos. You'll only end up hurt and wondering what you did wrong."

"I'll keep your warning in mind. Thank you, Allen."

Dinner moved along swiftly, and the conversation changed from Carlos to Pearson Computers and the local news stories of the day. Crystal was waiting for the opportune time to excuse herself and escape to the solitude of her bedroom. She wanted to call Gloria and catch up on what was happening in Corner Brook.

Once back in her room, Crystal dialed Gloria's number. When she heard Gloria at the other end, it brought tears to her eyes.

"Hi, Gloria, it's Crystal. How are you?" Crystal tried to hide the quiver in her voice.

"Crystal, it's so good to hear from you! I'm doing fine. My arthritis has been acting up and giving me some pain, but it hasn't been too bad so far this year. Nothing I can't handle."

"How is Samuel?" Crystal inquired.

"Samuel is doing great. He's been going to AA regularly and hasn't touched a drop since before he was arrested. It's made it easier for me to live with him, and he's still holding down his job at the mill. He misses you – I know that. He seems to be happy. I'm happier with him since he's stopped drinking. How have things been for you? Do you like living in Calgary? Do you have any plans to visit here?"

"Things have been fine for me. I just got back from a month of traveling in Europe with Carlos Zambeni as his assistant. It was a whirlwind trip, but fun. Lots of parties and such. It was hectic and vastly different from the quiet life of Corner Brook. Have you seen Michael and Katie? How are they doing?"

Gloria's voice stopped. It seemed like they had been disconnected. "Gloria, are you still there?"

"Strange you should bring them up. I'm not sure what happened to them. I hadn't heard from Michael about babysitting. I went over to the house, and everything was closed up tighter than a drum. The curtains were drawn. There's no sign of life around anywhere. Someone is looking after the mail, newspapers, and lawn.

Michael and Katie are nowhere to be found. I went to the police station, and all they would tell me was Michael has taken an extended leave of absence. They didn't know when he would be back. It's very strange to say the least. I would've thought he'd have stopped in to say goodbye. Samuel received a notification that he was to report to another officer until further notice, and that's all I know. I was going to ask you if you had heard from him or knew what happened to them."

"That's very strange indeed. I haven't spoken to Michael since before I left for Europe. It wasn't a very amicable conversation. Michael told me not to call anymore. I hope everything is okay with them." Crystal said concerned.

"Yeah, me too. It's very confusing why he would up and leave like that without telling anyone where they were going," Gloria replied.

Gloria and Crystal chatted about other things, and then the conversation ended. "If you hear anything, let me know," Crystal said before hanging up the telephone.

Crystal went downstairs to the kitchen and started to make herself a cup of tea. Maria could be heard giggling and whispering with someone down the hallway. Crystal knew Maria and Allen liked to spend time together, and she didn't want to interrupt.

She replayed the conversation with Gloria in her mind. What had happened to Michael and Katie? Where had they gone? She thought.

Crystal realized she knew very little about Michael and his life. She hadn't bothered to ask questions about things like whether he had family, what he did in his spare time and where he liked to go on vacation. She only knew he was a widower with a young daughter and worked at the local police station. All they had talked about was her past; he had not revealed much information to her about his own. She didn't know if he had brothers, sisters, or parents, or where they lived. She remembered Katie mentioning a grandmother and a pony. She wasn't sure whether they were real or made up since the passing of her mother. Maybe he had taken Katie on an extended vacation.

Crystal tried to shake the uneasy feeling she was beginning to feel after talking to Gloria. It was hard to imagine not being able to talk to Gloria to find out how Michael and Katie were doing. He had exited her life without a trace as quickly as he had come into it.

It was time for her to get a place of her own, she thought. Maybe she should branch out and leave both lives behind her. She had been happy working as a waitress. She could do that in Calgary just as easily as when they had lived in Pembroke. She was good at it and enjoyed the interaction with all the different types of people that would visit the diners and truck stops. It was time for her to stop listening to what everyone else wanted her to do and do what she felt was right for her.

As she undressed and slid between the sheets, she decided that was exactly what she was going to do. In the morning, she would start looking for a place to live and a new job. The corporate world was not where she belonged. It was not who she had been raised to be. She had been under Samuel's influence for twenty years. She could take care of herself. It was time she started doing so.

Chapter 10

CRYSTAL ALMOST JUMPED OUT OF bed. Today, she was going to start to be who she was and not what others wanted her to be. She dressed in clean jeans, an orange tank top and running shoes. She bounced down the stairs with enthusiasm. She stepped into the kitchen just in time to catch Maria and Allen sneaking a little hug before he left for work. They both parted like they had experienced an electric shock.

"Don't let me interrupt! I've known about the two of you since I moved in. It's hard not to notice the way you two look at each other. Why the big secret?" she asked.

Allen stepped forward. "Crystal, please don't let on to Mother and Dad that you know. Mother would be furious if she found out about Maria and me. We've been seeing each other since Maria started working here. That's why I never date. My heart belongs to Maria," Allen stated.

"Your secret is safe with me, Allen. Who am I to tell you

who you can have a relationship with? If she makes you happy, then that's who you should be with."

Allen's eyes showed how grateful he was for Crystal's discretion. "Thank you. Looks like you've decided to take the day off."

"Yes, sort of. I have errands to run and would like your help in buying a car. I'd like to have my own wheels. It's time I learned to drive in the city. There's lots to see and do, and the limo isn't always available. Besides, I don't like being chauffeured around all the time. I'd like to start driving again."

"I have time late this afternoon. How about I call you when I'm finished my last meeting. I'll take you to a place I know," Allen replied.

"I don't want a fancy sports car. I want a car that's dependable and mechanically sound. That's all. I don't want something that'll take me from zero to sixty miles per hour in seconds."

"Suit yourself. I know exactly where to take you. I have to be on my way, or I'm going to be late for my meeting," Allen said as he gave Maria a peck on the cheek before he left.

"Can I borrow your car, Maria?" Crystal asked, walking towards the foyer.

"Certainly, Miss. The keys are in my coat pocket. I'll get them for you," Maria replied.

Crystal hopped into Maria's little Kia and drove down the driveway. It felt good to be driving and on her own. She drove down Blackfoot Trail looking for a diner where she might be able to find a job.

It wasn't long before she spotted exactly what she was

looking for and hoped it would be her next employment opportunity. It was your typical everyday diner. There were glass windows across the front, and she could see the patrons sitting and chatting inside. These types of places were constantly looking for help. She would do whatever she could to be working and earning her own paycheque again.

Crystal opened the door to the diner and stepped inside. There was a long lunch counter with stools and a half dozen booths lining the wall along the plate-glass windows. Construction workers, truck drivers, and delivery men and women sat talking about the latest sport scores and news events. The conversations were quick and funny, and the voices she heard were louder and more relaxed than the places she had been in lately.

Crystal ambled over to the cash register and approached the waitress, who was dressed in a light blue uniform and had just finished with a customer's tab. "I'm looking for a job if you have anything available," Crystal inquired. "I wait tables and have been doing so for about five or six years. Do you need a hand?"

The waitress stepped out from behind the counter. She was an older woman with gray hair covered in a hairnet. She eyed Crystal up and down over the top of her horn-rimmed glasses and smiled. "I think we could use you. You're a cute little thing, spry looking. When can you start?"

"I can start tomorrow," Crystal said, smiling. "Is that soon enough?"

"That's fine. Be here by five in the morning. We open early. My name is Ruby and I'm the owner. Welcome to Ruby's Diner."

"See you in the morning Ruby, and thanks," Crystal said as she turned and walked out the door.

Crystal drove towards a basement suite for rent she had found on the Internet. The tiny one-bedroom sounded like it was exactly what she needed. She was crossing her fingers that it wasn't in a rough area of the city. The online ad described the apartment as a basement walk-out with south-facing windows. It sounded bright and cheery. She pulled into the driveway of the address she had written down. It was a lovely two-storey split entry on a quiet cul-de-sac. She knocked at the door and a young woman of about thirty answered.

"Can I help you?" she asked with an inquisitive look on her face.

"I'm Crystal Pearson. I called about the apartment. I was wondering if I could see it?"

"Oh yes, come in. My name is Belinda Young. Give me a minute, and I'll take you through it. I want to check on the baby first," she replied, as she disappeared.

Crystal waited inside the door and could hear Belinda quietly open and close a door down the hallway. She was as short as she was round. Her rainbow-coloured hair was cropped short to her head, and she wore a variety of different sized hoops in her ears. Her hazel eyes looked tired from long hours of looking after the baby asleep in the other room.

"I wanted to make sure he was still sleeping before I went downstairs," she whispered. "We have to go outside, as there's no entry from the main floor to the apartment downstairs. We closed it off when we moved in so we could use the space for an apartment and tenants could have their own private entrance. You'll have a fully equipped kitchen and laundry. There's one bedroom, the windows face south, and there's a walk out into the back garden. Do you work nearby?"

"I work at Ruby's Diner, not far from here."

Belinda nodded and continued. "The apartment is fully furnished, and you can change whatever you like. If you do any major changes like painting, it'll have to be put back to the way it was before you leave. While you're living here, though, you're welcome to make it your own."

Crystal followed Belinda around the side of the house and through a back door. The living room was extra large, and there were sliding glass doors leading to a lovely English garden. There were Adirondack chairs sitting under a towering maple tree and a manmade lily pond with a waterfall that bubbled and gurgled as the water made its way to the bottom of the rocks. There were walkways made of patio stones intertwined through the garden. Dozens of varied species of flowers of different colours grew at different heights. It was a private oasis tucked away in a residential city area.

"The rent is eight hundred a month, including utilities. What do you think?" Belinda looked at her with encouragement.

"I'll take it. I brought my damage deposit and first month's rent. I'd like to move in right away if that's okay?"

"I'd like that. I'll get you a receipt. I live here alone with the baby most of the time. My husband is in the Canadian Armed Forces and is away. Your name sounds familiar.

149

Should I know who you are, Crystal?"

Crystal smiled and briefly explained her history. Belinda nodded in acknowledgement as she remembered seeing the story on the news.

"I've found it tough adjusting to my new family and their lifestyle. I want to be on my own for a while," Crystal said.

"I can understand. Take the keys with you and move in whenever you want. I must get back upstairs in case the baby wakes up."

Crystal took the keys and held them in her hand looking at them for a few minutes. This was the first time she had ever lived in a place of her own. She walked to the car and drove back to the mansion to pack her suitcases.

The drive back to the Pearson house made Crystal feel more empowered than ever before. She could do this; she could strike out on her own. Samuel was in a serious relationship with Gloria, and she didn't have him to worry about any longer. Michael had told her not to call him again, so she decided to put the past behind her. There had to be someone out there somewhere for her.

She pulled up in front of the house and parked Maria's car where she had found it earlier in the day. She was excited about car shopping. It was also the first time she would own her own car. Crystal entered the house through the back door to find Maria. "Here are your keys, Maria," she said, dropping the keys on the counter. "Thank you for letting me use the car. I filled it up with gas on the way back, so you have a full tank."

Crystal left the kitchen and went out to see Jonathan in the greenhouse. She opened the door to see him standing on a ladder, watering the hanging Boston ferns. He turned to look at her as she shut the door behind her.

"Hi, Crystal. What brings you down here this afternoon? I thought you'd be at Zambeni Modeling clearing out your desk."

"No, I'm planning to go and clean out my desk tomorrow. I've decided not to take another job at Pearson. I have a job as a waitress in a diner. I feel so out of place in offices. I'm not the type of person to sit at boardroom tables arguing over portfolios and making corporate decisions. I've been a waitress pretty much since I left high school. I'm not confident enough to think I can walk into Pearson Computers and know what I'm doing. I also don't want to waste my time learning. It's not what I want to do. Right now, I don't know what I want to do, but one thing I do know is that the wheeling and dealing of the corporate world is not for me."

Jonathan stepped down off the ladder and sat on a nearby stool. "I see you're beginning to see things my way. I never liked it either. Amanda is almost obsessed with Pearson Computers. She threw herself into the company to keep her mind off losing you. I let her. She seemed to come naturally to it. I found it easier to spend my time here in the greenhouse and be Amanda's sounding board. We talk about everything that happens, but I rarely make an appearance in the boardroom. I like it that way. I'm much happier out here among the plants.

I like that you've decided to strike out on your own and make your own way in the world. It will help you build character. There are some very evil people in the world, Crystal. I know you don't think Samuel is one of them, but he was very evil. He took our daughter.

I do have to commend him, though, for doing such an excellent job teaching you right from wrong and helping you develop such a good and generous nature. It's something you wouldn't have learned from your mother. That still doesn't excuse what he did to you and to this family. Had you not been kidnapped, though, I doubt the business would have expanded the way it did. I didn't have the drive to be overly successful. Your mother had enough for both of us after you disappeared, and she really made the company what it is today.

There are all kinds of ways of looking at different situations and scenarios, but we must work with the cards we're dealt. If you're not happy working at the company or working for Carlos, you need to do what makes you happy. I'll support you in whatever you do."

Crystal bent over and gave Jonathan a kiss on the cheek. "Thank you, Jonathan. What you've said means a lot me. I knew I'd have your support. I really must go and meet Allen. He's going to take me shopping for a car," Crystal said as she turned and left him among the foliage.

Allen was already in the foyer waiting for her when Crystal came up the path from the greenhouse. "I was down talking to Jonathan about a few things. Sorry to keep you waiting."

"No worries. I'm ready when you are."

The two of them walked out the door and got into Allen's car. "I want something dependable and not flashy. Something not too expensive and a couple of years old."

"I'll take you to a friend of mine who owns a used car

dealership not too far from here. I'm sure he'll have something on the lot to suit you."

Allen turned his Saab into the lot and stopped. He got out of the car and said, "You have a look around. I'll go inside and find Jack."

Allen came out of the building with a tall, middle-aged man dressed in tan khakis and a white golf shirt. He had short, dark hair and was very thin for his stature.

"Jack, this is my sister, Crystal. She needs a car," Allen was saying as the two of them approached her.

"Hi, Crystal. It's nice to meet you. I'm sure I have exactly what you're looking for. Come take a look at this one," he said, pointing towards a little blue Toyota in the corner.

"It's a 2012 Toyota Matrix, 5-door hatchback in mint condition. It's a 1.8L, four-cylinder with great fuel economy at thirty-five miles per gallon. It has an automatic transmission, power steering and windows, and is equipped with air conditioning. It just turned ninety-five thousand kilometers and has been well cared for. It's spacious and is a dependable little vehicle," he said looking at her.

Crystal followed Allen around the car as Jack opened the driver's door so they could look inside. Crystal slid into the front seat and sat behind the wheel. It felt comfortable and right for her. She looked at Allen and laughed. "This seems too easy. I'll take it."

When the paperwork was complete, Jack handed Crystal the keys. "There you go. If you have any problems or questions, here's my card – give me a call. I'll look after you."

"Thank you very much," Crystal said, sliding behind the wheel and turning the ignition.

As she drove towards the Pearson house, Crystal felt a wave of peacefulness wash over her. She had been feeling so out of sorts, and for the first time in a long time she was starting to feel like her old self again.

She pulled into the yard and parked. It was getting close to dinner, and she needed to join the family in the dining room. She went to her room and quickly showered and changed. She tied her hair back in a ponytail, as there was no time to blow dry and fuss with it. She pulled on a clean t-shirt and wiggled into her freshly washed jeans. Flip flops would have to do, and she stepped into them.

She ran down the stairs, arriving in the dining room doorway out of breath. "Sorry I'm late," she said. Jonathan, Amanda, and Allen all turned to look at her as she quickly sat in her place at the dining room table. Amanda's expression told her she was not impressed with her appearance for dinner, but she remained silent.

Maria started serving the Waldorf salad, and Amanda started the dinner table conversation. "Allen says he took you to buy a car today, Crystal. It's nice that you feel comfortable enough in the city to drive on your own."

"Yes, I wanted something I could depend on to drive back and forth to work, do my own errands, and take a drive if I wanted to," she replied.

"When do you expect you'll be ready to return to work at Pearson?" Amanda questioned her.

"I'm not coming back to Pearson. I'm also leaving my job with Carlos. I found a position more suitable for me, more in line with what I'm used to doing. I don't like working in the corporate world. Since I've been in Calgary, I've realized more and more that the lifestyle you lead is not one I want for myself. Not that I have anything against the way you live, it's just not the way I was raised and not who I am.

I must admit when I first arrived it was all so overwhelming and captivating. Having a credit card with no limit, the idea of being able to travel all over the world, and go to parties and social galas with high profile people has been quite hypnotizing. But as time went on, I realized it wasn't where I wanted to be.

I enjoy contact with everyday people. I like to talk and socialize when I'm working. I've been a waitress for the past four or five years. I enjoy trying to make someone smile during the day. Having them comment on how great the food was, learning about where they're from and getting to know the regulars who come in every morning for coffee on their way to work.

I like the idea of standing on my own two feet. Now that I know who I am and that Samuel was not my Uncle Frank, how I feel about things has changed. I'll always love everyone here. You're my family, but I'm not like you. I've lived differently and was raised differently. Whether that ends up being a good thing or a bad thing, it's reality.

I have to travel my own path and make my own way. I've rented a place and have a position at a diner where I start tomorrow. I'm not comfortable living in this type of environment. I like to do things for myself. I'm not used to people waiting on me hand and foot. I realize this may be a lot for you to take in at once, but you'll adjust to not having me around as much. I'll come by to visit, and you're more than welcome to visit me, but I have to do this for myself."

Allen spoke up. "Well, I certainly didn't see this coming. I thought you liked living here."

"I do like living here," Crystal replied. "I just need to be on my own to figure things out. I can't do that while living here. I need a place of my own with my own things around me. I need to be able to know I can look after myself. These past years Samuel has been looking after me. Then, I went from living with him to living with you. Here, I have even more people looking after me and telling me what they feel is best for me. I don't even know what's best for me. I've never made any of my own decisions. I need to live on my own, get a feel for who I am and start looking at a future that's right for me, not what everyone else thinks is right for me. That doesn't mean I want to break all ties with my family. I really have two families. I miss Samuel and Gloria. I know Michael doesn't want to talk to me anymore, but I still miss him and Katie."

Amanda listened carefully and finally cleared her throat to interrupt Crystal's conversation so she could talk.

"When we came to get you, we had a deal that you would be with us for a year. Barely any time has passed. Now you want to move out on your own? You and I haven't had a chance to get to know each other, and you have spent very little time working at the company. How do you know it's not what you want to do?

While living with us, you can have everything you want. The world is at your fingertips. There isn't a young woman on the planet who wouldn't give up their present life to lead the life laid at your feet. You snub it like it's yesterday's trash. I can't believe you'd do this to us. We've done nothing to harm you. We've let you adjust to our way of life and have offered you nothing but wonderful things and opportunities. I'm beginning to think you had no intention of living with us for a year. I don't know what to say."

Crystal tried to put some compassion in her voice as she replied to Amanda. "I'm sorry, Amanda. There's nothing I can say that will ease your pain and change your thinking about me. I'm not like you. I can't see myself as a corporate executive. I'm not interested in holding a position for the sake of holding a position and having other people do my job for me. That's how I felt when I was traveling with Carlos. Other people were doing everything for me and even though it was supposed to be training for me, there was no training.

The conversations were secret between him and Ava, and I was kept out of the loop. I understand there are a lot of corporate secrets that no one wants to reveal to me right now, but I'm not interested in taking up space in an office until that time comes. I don't like to dress up every morning. I've never been a nine-to-five girl. I like to dress down, as you call it, and am comfortable in my jeans and sneakers. I like real people, not those who look at you and smile, then when your back is turned say nasty things about you.

Please try to understand that the world you live in is not the world I was brought up in. It certainly isn't a world I want to be a part of. The idea of having money is marvelous, but it's something I'm not used to. I've never been able to walk into a store and not look at price tags. I've had to scrimp and save for everything. In the scheme of things, I'm grateful for having done so, as I appreciate the things I have more. I worked hard to stay afloat while growing up, to help Samuel make ends meet. It seemed difficult at the time, but to tell you the truth I miss it.

I miss living a real life. I miss the bargain bins, yard sales, poking around flea markets. Walking into a store and being able to buy anything off the rack doesn't really appeal to me. It's no fun. There's no feeling of accomplishment like when you find that perfect item at a yard sale or in a bargain bin. I know it's hard for you to understand, but that's the way I feel. I have some money saved. I've already rented an apartment, and now I have a car. I'll furnish my place with second-hand items, pick up some odds and ends from yard sales and online. It will come together. It might not be what I'm used to here, but it will certainly be the kind of life I was used to living with Samuel. We always left whatever we had behind and started out gathering stuff when we moved into new towns. We've never had the same stuff sitting around all the time. I liked that.

Here, there's no change. Every day is almost exactly like the day before. We all get up and go to work in the morning. There are meetings, luncheons, dinner parties and social events. We come home, and Maria looks after things. There's never anything to do yourself. Everything here is done for you. When I tried to put my own dishes in the dishwasher it was frowned upon. You said we have people to do that for us. I can't get used to dressing up and being at a sit-down family dinner every night. When I was living with Samuel there were nights when I sat in front of the television with a bowl of Kraft Dinner and a glass of milk. In fact, until this very moment, I didn't realize how much I missed Kraft Dinner.

The meals here are like eating in a restaurant all the time.

There are no leftovers, and there is no such thing as cooking something for myself. I need to be in an environment where I feel comfortable. I can't relax here. I'm always on edge. I'm continually thinking I might not be doing something right and will be doing something that may upset you."

Jonathan nodded as Crystal explained how she felt about living at the house and her need for getting a place of her own. He knew what she was talking about. She could see it in his eyes. He felt the same way. He retreated to his greenhouse to escape the pressures of having to go to the office, of having to deal with the everyday life that being in the corporate world commanded. He liked to spend his days with his plants. He hated going to the parties and having to smile and be nice to people he knew were only interested in talking to him because of what they could get from him. He had been around the block enough to know that.

Jonathan cleared his throat. "Crystal, I commend you for what you're about to do. It's important that people make their own way in the world and do what's right for them. In hindsight, it was a mistake to ask you to come here and live with us. We should've left you in Corner Brook. It was wrong for us to uproot you and move you here to live with us. If you'd like to return to Corner Brook, I'd be more than happy to make those arrangements for you. The only thing I want is for you to be happy."

"Thank you, Jonathan. I'm quite content living in Calgary and being close to my family. I'm just not happy living in the same household. Thank you for understanding," Crystal replied gratefully.

Dinner continued quietly. Nothing more was said.

Amanda was stunned that she couldn't entice Crystal with wealth and power. Allen didn't like the idea of his sister working at a diner as a waitress and not knowing what kind of riff raff she would encounter. The streets of Calgary were dangerous. He knew all too well what could happen to someone as naïve as Crystal who didn't know how many people would target her as an easy mark.

Jonathan was sorry to know she would be leaving the house, yet he admired her courage for walking away and doing what she needed to do without their financial support. She had become a strong, independent young woman living with Samuel.

Once the meal was finished, Crystal left the table and went upstairs to pack. She was surprised to see her suitcases were standing neatly in the middle of the room. Maria had overheard the conversation and had gone upstairs and packed Crystal's things. She knew it was not Maria's intention to make her feel like she should be on her way immediately, but she couldn't help it.

Crystal went back downstairs to the kitchen. "Thank you, Maria, for packing my things. Could you have them brought down and put in my car please?"

"Not a problem, Miss. We'll miss you. I hope you'll be happy in your new life."

Crystal went to the living room where everyone was in the middle of a hush-hush conversation. It stopped immediately when Crystal entered the room. "Maria has seen to my belongings and is having them brought down and put into the car. Thank you again for understanding. I'll be in touch once I'm settled."

Crystal turned and walked towards the door. There were no hugs, no farewells. It was a matter-of-fact exit. She realized as she shut the door behind her that there was no warmth in this family. No one, including Jonathan, seemed happy. This was not what she wanted for herself. She checked the trunk to make sure her luggage was there, then slipped smoothly behind the wheel, turned the key, and drove out the gate and onto the street. Crystal felt a sense of freedom she had never felt in her life before. She turned the radio volume up as she drove down MacLeod Trail to her new home and her new life.

Chapter 11

MICHAEL WAS SPENDING HIS TIME getting to know Allen and trying to put together a business deal with Donavan. He was trying to convince him to invest in his real estate venture while getting close to learn as much as possible about his operation.

His main objective was to gain Donavan's trust to find out who Donavan and Carlos were, keep an eye on Crystal, and get her to return to Corner Brook. He was learning about Donavan and his connection to Carlos and that there was more to their businesses. He was beginning to suspect that one of them may be Dreamweaver, the man who had killed his wife and his partner. Dreamweaver had been a thorn in Michael's side almost since the day he started at CSIS.

Michael had left CSIS before he could catch Dreamweaver. When his wife died, he took Katie and moved to Newfoundland to start over where no one knew him. He made sure his mother was safely tucked away in Nova Scotia. He rarely went to see her in case someone caught on to who he was and put her life in danger.

It was hard living in a self-imposed protection program. He was certain Dreamweaver was behind the death of his wife and his partner, but he hadn't been able to gather the evidence he needed before he'd decided to leave CSIS. This was the only type of life Michael would ever know unless he could discover who Dreamweaver was and put him behind bars.

The last Michael knew of Dreamweaver, he was operating out of British Columbia, not Alberta. When Crystal's family came and moved her to Calgary, he had to follow. Michael did not want to see Crystal get tangled up in some sort of trouble.

He checked the backgrounds of all the Pearsons and their employees. There was nothing out of the ordinary. The history of the family was simple: a family of four who'd lost their daughter and had never given up looking for her. In the meantime, they had built a computer company empire that, according to market speculation, could some day rival Microsoft.

Allen was groomed to work at Pearson and take over when Amanda retired. He spent his time with executives on the golf course and at luncheons, dinners, and corporate events in the evening. He was never seen with a woman and didn't seem to date.

Allen was a young man who had grown up with parents who gave him the liberty to do anything he wanted. He was popular because of who he was. When he went to university, his parents were over-protective and closely monitored his academics. His mother nagged him to do well so one day he could step into her shoes and run the company.

Allen had graduated on the Dean's List. He had returned home and had immediately started to work for Amanda, gaining new clients who would be interested in using their computer software. The program Allen had designed was simple and easy to use. It had taken off like a shot, and Pearson Computers had become a company to be reckoned with on the world stage.

Now, he socialized all day. He spent his time marketing their innovative programs by attending every major event in the country and keeping abreast of the many new computer programmers looking for work in the industry. Allen was a firm believer in utilizing new young talent. He believed it was where the future lay for Pearson Computers. The young people had the ideas, used the programs, and would figure out where improvements could be made.

Allen capitalized on new talent. It had made the company a lot of money, much to the pleasure of his mother. Amanda wasn't happy with how much time Allen spent drinking and partying. She made that perfectly clear to him.

Michael and Allen had swiftly become friends and were spending time on the golf course together. Allen was friendly and easy to get along with. He had a style and personality that drew people to him. Michael thought from the first time he met Allen that he was on the up and up yet moved in very shady circles. This was beneficial for Michael. It was these types of circles Michael had to connect with to find

Dreamweaver. Michael was hoping the luck he'd had when he first arrived would hold out.

Allen was anxious for Michael to meet his sister, Crystal. There had been more than once when Allen had tried to encourage Michael to drop by the house when Crystal was home. Allen kept saying she was a great girl and the assistant to Carlos Zambeni, who ran the top modeling agency in the city. Allen was happily trying to plan an accidental meeting.

When Michael didn't seem overly anxious to meet Crystal, Allen questioned him on his relationship status. "Are you seeing someone? Are you married? I never see you with a woman. Are you gay?" Michael chuckled and told Allen he'd had a bad break-up and was not over it.

Allen was pushy about being introduced to Donavan. Donavan was one of the largest nightclub owners in the province. Allen was almost salivating at the thought of being able to provide Pearson Computer components and software programs for Donavan's nightclub security and other ventures. Allen insisted he didn't need much time to talk to Donavan. All he needed was an introduction at a social event or to have his name mentioned in a meeting. He was hoping Michael would be able to provide an opening to introduce himself. Allen was sure once he had the opportunity to talk to Donavan, he could convince him to have a sit-down meeting to present his ideas.

Michael picked up the phone and dialed his mother's number. It had been a while since he had spoken to her. He wanted to check on Katie. He had people working around his mother's farm for protection should they need it. He could tell a lot from the way she talked to him.

"Hello," Virginia's cheery voice came over the phone.

"Hi Mom, it's Michael."

"Michael, how wonderful to hear from you! How are things going? Are you coming for a visit soon? Did you find that lovely young lady you were looking for?"

"I'm still working on it. How are things going there? How's Katie?"

"Katie is off riding Midnight with the neighbour's daughter. They've been riding the trails almost every day. Her riding skills are really improving. She's having a fun time. I've enrolled her in some community organizations with children her own age. She needed to make friends and have someone to play with. I hope you don't mind. I had everything checked out thoroughly by the people you have working here. I wanted to make sure she would be safe. People in the community know she's my granddaughter, and I've hired help because of my age. They drive her into town and wait for her until she's done and return her home. Don't worry Michael, I wouldn't put her in any kind of danger. She needs some sort of normalcy to her life while she's here."

"Mom, what a wonderful idea and thank you! I'm happy she's having a social life there. I didn't expect to be this long, and I'm not sure how much longer I might be. This way she has friends, and it keeps her mind off being away from home."

"She asks about you all the time. I tell her you're working and trying to find Crystal. She's happy and doesn't complain. She's an angel, Michael – she always has been. She can stay here for as long as you need. You know she'll be safe with me.

Tell me what's happening in Alberta. Are you getting closer to finding Crystal? Are you getting closer to finding out who Dreamweaver is? Does anyone there know who you really are or why you're there? If so, be careful. I can't stress enough how dangerous it was for you when you first started chasing this guy. He knew everything about you at the end of it."

"Yes, he did, didn't he? I'm hoping I've been out of the spotlight long enough that he thinks I might have given up. Maybe he thinks I'm dead. That wouldn't be such a terrible thing either. I'm still working on it. I've found Crystal but haven't connected with her. I know where she's living and what she's doing. That's as far as I want to take it right now. I don't want to be connected with her if things get messy. The best thing I can do for her right now is stay away. Once I'm finished my investigation, I'll try to convince her to return with me. I don't know how successful I'll be, but I can hope."

Michael went over a few more things with his mother and hung up. They never stayed on the telephone long. It had always been a safety precaution to keep things short and to the point. He was supposed to meet Allen for lunch across the street, and he didn't want to be late. Allen was his only connection to Crystal.

Michael walked into the restaurant and immediately saw Allen wave from a booth along the wall.

"Hi there. I thought you may have forgotten. You're usually here waiting for me," Allen said as Michael sat down.

"Sorry about that – I was on the phone. The conversation ran longer than I planned. Thanks for waiting."

Michael ordered coffee and asked, "How ya been?"

Allen smiled and had obviously been drinking, even though it was early in the day.

"Not bad at all. Crystal made a shocking announcement last night. I'm still trying to digest it. I'm wondering what happened to make her decide to move out. I took her to buy a car yesterday, and then she announces she's found her own apartment and has taken a job as a waitress at a diner. It was all extremely fast and surprising to say the least."

"Did she say where she was moving to or working, or did she leave everyone in suspense?"

"She offered no details. She made the announcement and left. It was very unusual. I don't know her that well, so maybe it's not. She seems to have disappeared."

"Eventually she'll let you know where she is. Until then, there really isn't much you can do."

Michael made a mental note to contact Ed and have him follow up on Crystal. He wanted to make sure she was safe.

Allen interrupted his train of thought. "Do you think you know me well enough to set up a meeting with Donavan? I'd really like to be able to let him know Pearson Computers is more than capable of taking over the computers he has in his nightclubs."

"I'm going to be meeting with Donavan later. I'll ask him and see what his reaction is. He's just getting to know me. I don't want to spook him by adding someone else into the equation."

"No, I understand. Donavan is very careful about who he does business with. How about we meet later this week after your meeting with Donavan? You can let me know how he feels about getting together with me."

They finished their meal, and Michael left the restaurant with a million questions in his mind about Crystal. He thought he'd had a perfect connection to keep tabs on her and now she was gone.

Michael pulled out his cellphone and called Ed.

"This is Ed."

"Ed, Michael here. I need you to do some research for me on Crystal Pearson. She's moved out of the family home, found an apartment, and is working at a diner somewhere here in Calgary. I'd like to find her and put an undercover agent in close proximity to keep an eye on her."

"Sure, Michael. I'll see what I can find out and let you know. How are things going out there?"

"Nothing yet, but I think I'm on the right track and closing in. I've been meeting with Donavan Whitman. I think he's beginning to trust me. I'm meeting him later today and might not have a chance to call. I'll call the next chance I get."

Michael hailed a cab and gave him the address of the 2440 nightclub where Donavan ran his business during the day. The cab pulled up in front and Michael went inside. There was a big man inside the door who stopped him. "I'm here to see Donavan. Tell him it's Michael."

The man walked towards the back of the club and disappeared through a door. He returned and ushered Michael to follow him. Michael looked from side to side, rechecking the layout as he started forward. He always liked to make sure of his surroundings before entering someone's back office.

Michael stepped over the threshold to the back room.

Donavan sat at a desk facing the door. The room was furnished in dark wood and deep, rich reds. It was smaller than Michael expected for someone of Donavan's reputation. There was room enough for Donavan and two or three other people.

Donavan motioned for Michael to sit down. He glanced around the room, taking in his surroundings. There was a man standing at the door waiting for instructions to stay or leave. Donavan motioned for him to leave, and he shut the door on his way out.

"Michael, it's good to see you again. I've been checking into your operation. You have quite the reputation for knowing what's happening with real estate. I have to be incredibly careful when meeting new people and who I'm entering into business with. I must make sure I know who they are and what their intentions are. I haven't come this far in my business by being reckless."

"I understand. I'm the same way. In our business, you have to be careful. There are opportunities for us to make money. We need to take advantage of them when we see them. The real estate market in Calgary right now is the perfect place to expand and develop strategies to capitalize on a very lucrative market.

Alberta will come back in time. If you're not willing to wait for the return on your investment, then it's not a market for you. From what I've heard, you're a man who looks to the future and doesn't always put his eggs in one basket. Blocks of property can be snapped up for a song, and with the right partners and connections they could be turned into thriving communities designed for the younger generation.

Jobs could be created by the construction of these new communities and bring young families to the area. This in turn would be a way to increase the value of the properties and attract business. Attracting business attracts more families, and so on. Calgary is where the real estate market is going to boom in the next ten or fifteen years, and you have the connections necessary to help move it along easily.

There's been talk of setting up speciality communities to show off to the rest of the country. The city is on an upswing, and development around a specialty community could be extremely lucrative. It could turn out like Florida in the sixties, where communities were built to lure retirees for the winter months. Florida's population almost doubles during the winter. Canadians have become an industry in Florida. My business associates and I think its time to do the same thing in Alberta.

Real estate is unbelievably cheap for anyone who wants to go in and purchase large parcels of property and start building tiny homes. There is an opportunity to open night clubs, restaurants, coffee shops and stores of all kinds. If done properly, you could almost build your own city of tiny houses outside of Calgary.

It's a short drive to the American border and British Columbia. I've been watching the popularity of tiny homes. They could offer excellent returns for those willing to take a chance. You must admit, there are few areas in the real estate market where the infrastructure is already in place."

Donavan watched and listened to Michael, considering every word he was saying. There was merit to his argument. The price of real estate in Calgary was rising almost daily.

If he was going to get in on any last-minute deals before housing and land prices increased, he would have to start investing now. Michael was right. It was the perfect time to expand his real estate holdings and business ventures.

"Let me bring you a full proposal of an area I've been watching. There are buildings that could be renovated and restored to accommodate your nightclub style. I'm sure it wouldn't be hard to attract a builder to the area, especially if there was enough work to last him and his crew a substantial amount of time. It would be easy for me to find everything you want and need to make this investment a success.

Another company you might be interested in looking at is Pearson Computers for the security of your businesses and the planned expansion construction sites. I met Allen Pearson my first night in the city. I was leaving the club and we bumped into each other. He gave me a ride back to my hotel. We've met on several occasions, and he seems like a knowledgeable young fellow. You may benefit from sitting down with him and discussing what he can do for you.

I've thought about approaching him with the real estate idea to see if their company might be interested in entering the real estate market. If positioned in the right area, Pearson Computers could build their own tiny house community to house not only their business, but also their staff."

Michael watched Donavan and tried to read his body language. Did he seem interested? Would he take the bait with Michael only being in Calgary to promote and market the ideas of building the tiny house community? Donavan nodded in acknowledgement. Michael could tell he was reflecting on what he was being told.

"I'm aware of Pearson Computers and their capabilities as a company. I've thought about approaching them and discussing my various business interests to find out exactly what they can offer me. I've heard remarkable things about them. Calgary is going to be hopping with construction and growth in the next ten years. I want to get in on the ground floor and capitalize on that expansion. Let me consult a few of my other investors. I'll get back to you. In the meantime, pass my contact information on to Allen Pearson. I'll sit down with him, too."

Michael took Donavan's last statement as his cue to leave. "I'll leave you then. Give me a call when you want to meet again."

Michael walked towards the door and turned the knob. It was a good meeting, he thought. He was slowly beginning to feel Donavan was starting to trust him. He was happy Donavan agreed to talk to Allen. Allen would be ecstatic. Their meeting may result in expanding Pearson Computers to manage Donavan's nightclubs and businesses.

Michael left 2440 and walked in the direction of his hotel. The weather was beautiful. He would enjoy the walk. He pulled out his cellphone and dialed Ed's number.

"Ed, here." His voice boomed on the other end.

"Ed, it's Michael again. I was wondering what you were able to find out about Crystal."

Ed chuckled. "It wasn't hard, Michael. She bought a car yesterday. I was able to gather all her information from the registration. I'm not sure where she's working. I have her under surveillance. My agent will follow her until he finds out. Don't worry, I have my best man out there tailing her.

We'll know everything tomorrow."

"Thanks, buddy. I appreciate your help. I'm moving along smoothly here. No indication from anyone that they suspect anything. I'll give you a call tomorrow."

Michael hung up and dialed Allen's number. Allen didn't answer. Michael left a message on his voicemail telling him he could contact Donavan for a meeting. He left a number Allen could call to set up the appointment.

Michael made his way back to the hotel and stretched out on the bed in front of the television. He would stay in tonight. It had been hectic, and he didn't want to be seen as a party boy in Calgary. Michael wanted people to assume he was only in town for business and nothing more. Finally, by midnight, he was tired enough to roll over and go to sleep.

Chapter 12

IT HAD BEEN ALMOST A month since Crystal had moved out of the Pearson house and started her job at Ruby's Diner. She spent her days off combing through second-hand stores, flea markets, and yard sales picking up odds and ends, kitchenware, dishes, pots and pans, and little decorative knick-knacks.

She relished her solitude. She enjoyed getting up in the morning and sitting at the small patio table in the garden with her coffee. In the evenings, she would change into her sweats and t-shirt and veg in front of the television watching chick flicks, comedy shows or surfing Netflix. Dinner might be a sandwich, a can of soup or a full-cooked meal.

She spent time getting to know Belinda and her son Matthew upstairs. Belinda's husband was in the Canadian Armed Forces and was currently serving in Afghanistan. He had been gone about two months and was not expected back until early in the new year.

They had been married about five years, and after much deliberation about children, they had decided to begin a family, even though they knew he would be required to do at least one more tour overseas. Belinda didn't know how she felt about being solely responsible for raising their children while he was away on duty, but she loved Nathan and wanted to have a family.

They'd met while Nathan was in basic training in St. Jean, Quebec, and had fallen madly in love. Belinda had been working for the summer as a cashier in a local convenience store which Nathan used to frequent. They'd struck up a conversation, and it wasn't long before he'd asked her out. They'd spent hours talking, and following his graduation from boot camp he'd asked her to marry him.

They moved about every two years, and he had quickly climbed the ranks. Belinda had been left on her own. It was not the life she had imagined when she married him. They stayed connected by email, Skype, and text messages. There had been a time or two before Matthew was born when she would travel to meet him in foreign places.

Belinda loved taking care of their son. You could tell by the look in her eyes and the way she lovingly cared for the baby that she was a wonderful mother and would do anything for her family. Once Matthew was in bed for the night, Crystal and Belinda would meet and sit in the garden to talk.

They chatted about what it was like growing up with Samuel and moving all the time, and how it had come as such a shock when Michael revealed the results of his private investigation into her background and found out her true identity.

Crystal told Belinda she and Michael had fallen in love and how much she enjoyed looking after and playing with Katie. As Crystal talked about Michael and Katie, she felt a tug at her heart. She had spoken to Gloria a couple of times to see if there had been any news on their whereabouts or if they had returned. Gloria always had to tell her there was no news, and Crystal continually wondered what had happened to the two of them. Gloria promised to call her as soon as anything new developed, but by the sounds of things, Michael and Katie had disappeared for good.

Crystal discussed with Belinda how hard it had been for her to find out Samuel was not her Uncle Frank, and how bad she had felt for him when she knew the whole story. She revealed she wasn't angry or upset; in fact, she felt she'd had a good upbringing, even though it wasn't the upbringing or life she would've led had she been living with the Pearson family. It was a good life, nonetheless.

One evening, as they were both enjoying a glass of German Riesling, she told Belinda about the trip to Europe with Carlos and how after their return to Calgary she had never heard from him again. "I guess Allen was right. He was just looking for a new ornament."

The belongings in her desk had been boxed and shipped to Pearson Computers with a note reading, 'Had a wonderful time. Unfortunately, Ava and I feel you'd be better suited for a different occupation. We appreciate your ideas on the natural woman look and are now using them in our ads. Best of luck in the future. Carlos'

Allen dropped the box off to her one afternoon on his way home from work. They sat and chatted about how she was missed at the family dinner table. Jonathan seemed to be the most affected by her absence. Amanda was still hurt by her exit but was happy she was living in the same city. There was always hope for Amanda and her to become closer if Crystal remained in Calgary.

Allen was excited about a new deal he was negotiating with Donavan Whitman, one of Calgary's biggest nightclub and real estate developers. His friend Michael had set up an introduction for him. Allen was sure the company would benefit extensively from the union. Allen suspected this new contract would increase their bottom line by almost a third of their total profits for the year. Amanda would be extremely pleased with him landing such a big client.

He and Maria were still an item, and he was wondering if he should try to explain to his mother that they were in love and wanted to marry. He wanted to spend the rest of his life with her. It would make it easier if they didn't have to sneak around the grounds. He wanted to be able to take Maria out with him. They wanted to travel together and openly display the love they shared for each other.

Allen wanted to know if Crystal thought he should approach Jonathan first in the same way she had done when she was going to move out. He had been impressed by how Jonathan had supported Crystal and her decision to be her own person. Allen wanted to garner the same support if Crystal thought it might be a promising idea.

Jonathan understood more about having a personal life and how important it was to be with the people you love. Allen admitted Crystal had given him the courage to announce his long-standing love affair with Maria. He hoped Crystal had broken the ground for him to make his own announcement and move towards publicly starting a life with Maria.

Crystal thought about Allen making the announcement at the dinner table in the same shocking fashion that she had made her own. Amanda's reaction would most likely be more of the same condescending demeanour she'd shared when Crystal had told everyone she was leaving.

Amanda wanted her children's relationships to be more of a business merger than an emotional bonding, and she wouldn't be impressed with Allen wanting to marry the maid. Her biggest concern would be how it would look when one of the top business executives in the city was tying the knot with a member of their household staff.

Her first reaction would be to ask if Maria was pregnant. Allen didn't want to subject Maria to Amanda's wrath, but neither one of them could see any other way around it if they wanted to get married and start a family.

Crystal agreed that Amanda wouldn't take the news well. The only way for Allen and Maria to start a future together would be to tell Amanda and Jonathan. At least they wouldn't have to sneak around any longer.

"You must tell them, Allen. It's not fair to you or Maria if you're hiding around corners all the time. How do you think Maria feels knowing that you're afraid to tell your parents you love her? It can't make her feel particularly good about the situation."

"She says she doesn't mind. She understands. I just want

to be able to be with Maria all the time. The only way I'm going to be able to do that is if I tell Mother and Father. I could really use the moral support."

Crystal smiled and looked at her older brother. "I'll come over tomorrow night, if you think I'll be of any help to you. It's wonderful that you've finally decided to bring your relationship with Maria out into the open. I'd like to be there to see the look on Amanda's face when you tell her. She's going to think I put you up to it, you know."

Allen got up to leave and turned towards the door. "You seem really content here. Thanks for promising to come by tomorrow night."

Crystal closed the door behind him, washed the coffee cups and started to get ready for work. She enjoyed working at Ruby's Diner. There were the regulars who came in on their way to work in the morning, and she was getting to know them. They appreciated how fast she'd picked up on their regular morning coffee orders.

Ruby was impressed with how rapidly she'd learned the routine of the diner and how the customers liked her. She was friendly and liked to listen to their stories. She moved with ease through the diner juggling coffee pots, plates of food, and condiments. It was obvious she had spent many hours working in a diner environment.

Crystal and Ruby were getting along famously. Ruby made it a point not to become overly friendly with her staff, as it interfered in the employer-employee dynamics. Ruby had learned a long time ago it was better to keep her relationships with her employees strictly professional. There were no complications that way. Ruby was aware of Crystal's background and story. Crystal had been completely open about it. The story followed her wherever she went. Everyone recognized her from the news, and when they met her, it was always, "Haven't I seen you some place before?" She sometimes felt like a washed-up movie star who'd had one or two big films and then disappeared. Everyone recognizes them but can't put their finger on where they've seen them before.

The diner was a popular place in the morning. The little silver bell at the top of the door casing tinkled almost continually as people came and went for food or coffee on their way to and from work. It was a diverse crowd. There were truck drivers waiting for warehouses to open so they could unload their trailers and move on to the next stop, and construction workers responsible for a variety of jobs. There was a never-ending sound of work boots clomping on tile as they made their way to the counter stools or booths. Office workers dressed in business suits came to grab a quick breakfast because of a late morning start. People of all shapes and sizes moved through the diner daily.

Crystal liked the hustle and bustle of the diner. There was always laughter as someone told the joke of the day. There were others who wanted to have their morning coffee at a booth next to the window to read their paper and keep an eye on the traffic moving outside.

It was the interaction with people that Crystal enjoyed the most. She liked the stories of their families and getting to know who they were and where they were from. Everyone had a story. It wasn't long before Crystal knew them by name and knew exactly where they would sit and what they would order.

She knew who was battling the failure of a personal relationship and if someone had recently lost a loved one. They told her if their children were in trouble, if they were worried about their jobs, if they had found a new love or were planning to travel in the future. People opened up to her, and she seemed to gravitate to those who needed a bit of compassion or empathy to start their day.

The men coming in and out liked her. They flirted with her, asked her out, and teased her about having a secret lover. She never accepted any invitations; she wasn't interested. She'd had two failed relationships in a brief period and wanted a break.

At the end of her shift, she tucked her apron into a bag and put on an old black sweater she had found at a flea market. When she put it on, it gave her a warm, fuzzy feeling, and she wore it most of the time. It was old enough that the yarn had softened with age. It felt good against her skin.

When she stepped outside, the cool air felt good on her face. Fall was coming, and she was adjusting to life in Calgary. When she had first arrived in the city, she had found it hard to handle the dryness of the air because of the elevation.

Today, it was clear, and the Rocky Mountains could be seen towering in the distance. She unlocked her car and slid in behind the wheel. It had been a while since she had been to the Pearson house for dinner. It wasn't something she looked forward to. She knew Allen needed her support when he told Amanda and Jonathan about Maria.

Traffic was light on Deerfoot Trail, and Crystal felt a

knot developing in the pit of her stomach as she pulled through the gates at the Pearson estate. She was hoping Allen had told Maria she would be joining them for dinner. She didn't plan to stay, only long enough to eat, have Allen reveal his long-standing affair with Maria, and shortly thereafter make her exit. She rang the doorbell and stood waiting for someone to answer. The door opened, and Jacob stood before her.

"Hello, Miss. Come in. The family is waiting for you in the living room," he said, opening the door wider for her to enter.

Maria was serving cocktails when Crystal stepped through the living room door and attentively brought the tray to her when she sat down.

"It's good to see you, Miss. We've missed you around here," Maria said with a welcoming smile.

Amanda spoke sarcastically. "I see you've decided to come for a visit. It's nice you haven't forgotten who your family is in Calgary. I expected we'd see more of you than we have. What have you been doing with yourself that keeps you away so much?" Jonathan smiled at her and almost whispered, "I've missed you."

Allen stood leaning against the fireplace. It was obvious he'd had too much to drink. When he moved, you could see him trying to stabilize himself. She felt bad for Allen and wished he would get help with his drinking problem. Crystal took a mouthful of her drink and cringed as the fiery liquid slid down the back of her throat.

"I've been working six days a week. By the time I get

home, I'm exhausted. All I want to do is get into my PJ's and relax. I had forgotten that being a waitress can be such demanding work and how difficult it is being on my feet all day. Ruby is wonderful to work for. She's demanding, but fair. The clientele is fun to be around most days, and everyone I work with is great.

My landlord Belinda and I spend time together sitting in the garden chatting during the evenings after she puts Matthew down for the night. I've settled into a very nice routine that suits me well."

Maria stood in the doorway to let everyone know dinner was ready to be served, and the family made their way to the dining room. The meal started off with regular conversation surrounding the company and how Allen was making out with the real estate tycoon Donavan. He was excited about the prospect of bringing Donavan's business to Pearson. He was convinced it wouldn't be long before Pearson Computers would be installing all their software at the many nightclubs, warehouses, and corporate towers managed and owned by Donavan.

Allen was starting to focus on convincing Michael that Pearson Computers would be the prime computer company to be linked with the project in Calgary he was pitching to Donavan. He was encouraged by Michael's interest in the company and was hoping to soon have a contract in place for a sizeable expansion.

Amanda was leery about developing the company too fast. She was encouraged as Allen talked about Donavan and Michael's business successes. She was aware of who Donavan was, and was looking forward to meeting Michael soon. No contract would be signed without her approval.

Jonathan made very few comments during dinner. He sat, ate, and nodded at the appropriate times. Crystal watched him; it was like he was invisible. He hardly spoke a word. She felt sorry for him. He seemed so out of place and uncomfortable.

Allen cleared his throat and began to speak clearly and articulately. "I have an announcement to make. I'm glad you could be here, Crystal. I've decided to move into my own place and have purchased a condominium downtown closer to the office. When Crystal moved out, it got me thinking I should be on my own, too."

Amanda looked up from her dinner plate, put her fork down and picked up her wine glass before speaking. "You want to move out? I don't think that's a particularly good idea. You have everything you want here. You have Maria to wait on you and no expenses of your own. I don't think moving out would be a smart idea."

Allen looked at his mother. "It's time. I'm almost thirty years old and should have a place of my own. Also, Maria will be coming with me when I leave. She and I have decided to move in together. We've been seeing each other almost since she came to work for us. We'd like to be on our own and are considering getting married next year and starting a family."

Jonathan smiled. He knew Allen and Maria had been sneaking around the house. He hadn't said a word to anyone. He'd accidently come across them from time to time holding hands, laughing, and cuddling in the garden. He'd heard them in the hallways when they didn't suspect anyone else was around. He was happy for Allen. It was apparent the two of them were madly in love.

Amanda looked like someone had slapped her in the face. "I'm sorry, Allen, that won't do. There's no way I'll approve of Maria living with you and I'm certainly not going to accept the two of you getting married. I like Maria, but she's one of our staff. I'm sure you can do far better than the household maid."

Allen's smile disappeared. "I'm sorry you feel that way, Mother, but I'm old enough to make my own decisions, and this is one of them. You'll accept it or you won't, but it's going to happen."

"We'll see about that! I'm not going to have my son married to our housekeeper. If you decide to go ahead with your plans, then maybe you should think about looking for a position in another company," Amanda snarled.

Allen sat back in his chair and looked intently at his mother. "You'd fire me for wanting to be happy? I didn't think even you would stoop that low."

Jonathan hadn't said a word. He was sitting and listening to the conversation between Allen and Amanda. He quietly intervened.

"Amanda, let the boy go. The children need to be happy and need to be able to have lives of their own. You can't try to keep tabs on them twenty-four seven. You need to accept that they're not always going to make decisions you think are best. They're not children any longer. If Allen is in love with Maria and they want to be together, we're not going to stop them. To threaten Allen with his job if he doesn't do what you say is wrong, and as CEO I won't let that happen.

Allen is good for the company. He's been working hard to expand our operations and to increase the company's market value. Why would you want to fire him? That wouldn't make logical business sense. He would still be coming to the office. You'd see him there. We can find another maid. Why not leave it up to Maria to find her own replacement? I'm sure she knows someone suitable. We can't dictate who our children fall in love with. We must accept their choices and love them for who they are and what they become. Most of all, we want nothing more than for them to be happy. I know Maria will do everything in her power to make Allen happy.

There's no sense in causing unnecessary rifts in the family. Both children will be living close by, and we can see them whenever we want. If we make it difficult for them to have futures of their own and to live outside our home, how will they survive after we're gone? Let him go, Amanda. Let him be happy."

Crystal sat saying nothing. There wasn't anything she could say. She was there for moral support for Allen, but it was clear Jonathan had that covered.

Allen motioned to Maria to step forward, and he put his arm around her. "Maria and I love each other. I'm going to marry her. If you're not happy for us, then fine. A moving truck will be here tomorrow to load and take my belongings to my new place downtown."

Crystal stood up. "I have an early shift in the morning. It was wonderful seeing you all. Allen, I'm so happy for you and Maria. I'll visit once Maria feels she has everything organized. If there's anything I can help you with during the move, give me a call."

Crystal stepped forward and hugged them both. She went over and hugged Jonathan. Amanda held out both her hands and took Crystal's two in her own. "It was nice to see you, Crystal. Come for dinner anytime."

There was no warmth in her voice. Crystal left wondering how a person could be so cold and without feeling towards her own children. I'm glad Samuel was the parental figure in my life when it was most important. He was never this cold to me, she thought.

Crystal hopped in her car and drove out the driveway and into the traffic. She felt a sense of relief on the highway. She was a long way from Newfoundland and what she would call home and there was a little tug at her heart. I think I'm beginning to feel homesick if that is even possible for someone like me. But the home I knew wouldn't be the same without Michael and Katie, she thought as she drove back to her apartment.

Crystal continued to stay in touch with Gloria, and there was still no word on where Michael and Katie had disappeared to or if they were coming back. Gloria continued to ask around and had even driven by the house a few times. The place was locked up tight. Crystal was beginning to think she would never know what had happened to them.

Chapter 13

THE ALARM SEEMED TO SCREAM as Crystal hit the snooze button and rolled over. The morning shifts were the hardest. She hadn't slept well and had spent a good portion of the night tossing and turning. She crawled out of bed and made her way to the kitchen to start the coffee pot before going to take a shower. As much as she disliked the morning shift, she did like her job. There was a bustle of activity at the diner in the morning. She dressed in her pale blue uniform and headed out the door to the car. She noticed a different car in the yard and wondered who was visiting Belinda.

The diner was hopping when she arrived. The morning construction crew crowd was shuffling in. Crystal grabbed a coffee pot and started pouring refills as she made her rounds to take orders and say hello to those she knew. While doing so, she noticed a young couple she had never seen before. The girl didn't look more than twenty years old. The boy may have been a year or two older. Crystal walked up and gestured towards their coffee cups. "More coffee?" she asked. The girl nodded without saying a word or looking up as Crystal poured. "Can I get you anything else?"

"Nah, coffee's fine," the boy replied.

"If you change your mind, flag me down. I'll come back to check," she said, turning and walking away.

The girl was dressed in a black blouse, black jacket, and a short black ruffled skirt. The silver hooks on her knee-high, black boots sparkled like stars against the blackness of the laces binding the two sides of the boots together. Her pale white skin peeked through the numerous holes in the black fishnet stockings she wore. Around her neck was a black leather, silver-studded dog collar, and her straight, long, black hair hung in strands around the sides of her face. She wore black eye shadow and black lipstick. A number of places on her face were pierced with hooks, rings, and studs.

The boy was dressed in long baggy jeans that hung low enough to show his superhero underwear when he got up to go to the washroom. He wore a baggy white t-shirt, and his blond hair hung below the edges of a Calgary Stampeders ball cap turned backwards with the visor sitting at the nape of his neck. The Vans high-top sneakers he wore were used for riding the skateboard that was propped up beside the booth.

Crystal put her orders in to the line cook and then went to check with Ruby, who she thought might know the new couple.

"Ruby, who are the young couple sitting in the back booth? I haven't seen them before," she asked.

"That's Annette and Max. They come in once or twice a week. Netty, as she likes to be called, has been sick, and Max is always with her. He looks after her, or so I understand. I'm not positive on their backgrounds. You hardly ever see one without the other. Sometimes she sits and waits for him. He comes back to walk her home. They never eat anything. They only order coffee, sit for an hour or two, and go along their way. We've never had any problem with them. They're polite and pay their bill. I don't bother them. They seem like good kids."

Crystal delivered food to the patrons and once again grabbed the coffee pot to make her rounds. She approached the two and, without asking, started to pour them refills.

"I'm new here. I haven't seen the two of you before. You both look like you could use something to eat. Let me buy you breakfast."

Netty and Max looked up with expressions of disbelief on their faces. "No thanks. We don't take charity. If we eat, we pay," Max stated.

"It's not charity. It's the new girl buying you breakfast as a friendly gesture. We're about the same age. I like to treat my first-time customers. It establishes a good relationship between the waitress and patrons and encourages people to return another time. What do you say to bacon, eggs, hash browns, and toast to go along with that coffee?"

Netty and Max looked at each other. Crystal could see Netty wanted to agree and put something solid in her stomach.

"All right then. Just this once. Next time we buy our own," Max said.

"Oh, I'm only going to offer to do it once – don't worry about that. I can hardly afford to feed myself. Like I said, I like to do it for my first-time customers, and you two are first-time customers to me."

Crystal took the details of how they liked their eggs and sauntered off to hand the order in to the line cook window. "This one's on me, Vinnie," she said through the opening.

He looked at her and nodded. "You got it, Crystal."

Crystal continued to work, and as she did, she started to wonder what the story was surrounding the pair in the corner. They looked forlorn, and the sadness in Netty's eyes couldn't be hidden. Max was trying to portray himself as the tough protector. Crystal watched as they both emptied their plates in record time. They were trying to eat slowly, but the demands of their stomachs had overridden their ability to hide how hungry they really were.

When they were finished, Crystal walked over and started to take the empty plates. "Do you two live around here or come in often? I don't work the morning shift all the time. I'm here at various times of the day. What are your names?"

"I'm Netty and he's Max. We live down by the trestle bridge. I can only get out once or twice a week. I have fibro-myalgia, and sometimes I find it hard to walk far. I'll be rested up enough to make the trip home soon. We won't take up the booth for much longer."

"I'm sorry to hear that, Netty. I've heard that disorder can be very painful. You don't look like you've had much sleep. I hope the breakfast gives you some strength and you feel better. I'm new in the area and don't know many people. It's nice to come in and see a couple the same age as

I am. You take as long as you like. I'll pour you more coffee
and bring you some water in case you get caffeined out. I
know that if I drink too much coffee, I get the jitters. I must
get back to work. I'll look forward to seeing you again. Take
care," Crystal said and walked away.

About an hour after their breakfast, Crystal watched
Netty ease up slowly from the table as Max took her arm to
steady her and walk out the door. It was quite a responsibility for the young man to take on, and Crystal admired him
for doing so. She wondered what he did for work. She didn't
want to pepper them with too many questions for fear that
they may have found her too nosy and decided to avoid her.

She wished she knew how to contact them. She thought
with her new-found wealth she might be able to help them
out. She would have to come up with a cunning way to do
so. It was obvious they were determined not to take charity
and were hell-bent on supporting themselves.

As she was driving home, she suddenly realized how
much good she could do with the money that was available
to her. It gave her an idea. Helping others in some form
would be good public relations for Pearson Computers.
With all the money in the Pearson family, why not spread
some of the good fortune around? There were so many
people who could use a helping hand without feeling like
it was charity.

She called Allen as soon as she got home and ran the
idea past him. He was impressed with it, and they made
plans to get together and discuss in detail what was on her
mind. Allen said he would let Amanda in on what they were
looking at, and if she wanted to be a part of it, great. If not,

they would go ahead without her. He knew Jonathan would be thrilled with the idea of helping anyone that needed a lift.

Things for Allen had improved. He was elated living with Maria in their condominium downtown. Maria was happy not having to work for Amanda or hide her relationship with Allen. Allen had cut back on his drinking and seemed to be making a conscious effort to spend more time with Maria. He spent less time out drinking or making business deals over liquid lunches. Crystal was thrilled for both of them. She and Maria were becoming fast friends.

Amanda was adjusting to Allen having moved in with the hired help and was trying to accept Maria as part of the family. She was not pleased, but she was trying.

Jonathan was thrilled that Allen had finally given up the late nights of drinking and the friends he was associating with to settle down. He was hoping there would soon be a wedding and a grandson or granddaughter to complement the family.

Later that evening, Crystal was sitting in the backyard with a glass of white wine playing the events of the day back through her mind. She liked Netty and Max and wanted to help them if she could. Allen promised to drop by so they could talk. While she waited, Belinda came out in the yard to join her. Belinda looked drained as she sunk into the Adirondack chair beside her.

"You look exhausted, Belinda. Are you okay? I noticed a car in the driveway this morning. Is everything all right?" Crystal asked, concerned for her friend.

"My husband is back early from Afghanistan. I was so excited to see him. I had no idea he was coming home. We spent the entire night talking and catching up. The strange thing is, he seems different. I didn't want to say anything to him. I guess it might have to do with the fact we've been apart for so long. He's gone to the base to do some stuff with regards to his return. He'll be back later. He hasn't told me much. We talked about him being over there, but he said little about the mission and what he was doing, or why he's home early. I know some men died while he was there. It was on the news. They were from a unit in Ontario. I'm thankful he's back safe.

I'm probably being overly concerned. I've heard about soldiers after they've completed a couple of tours and how it affects them. He was saying last night that he didn't know if he could do it anymore and that worries me. What will we do if he doesn't have a job?

The military is all he knows. He joined when he was eighteen. We've never known any other kind of life. I don't have much training in anything, and now with the baby I don't want to have to leave him to go to work. I wouldn't even know what I'd do, and I don't know what Nathan would do. He's never done anything besides be a soldier."

Crystal touched her arm and replied, "Maybe it's the shock of him coming home and being here again. Why not let some time pass and see how things go? There's no sense worrying about something that may or may not happen. Can I get you a glass of wine?"

"Maybe you're right. I'm getting myself all worked up for nothing. Yes, please, I'd love a glass."

Crystal got up and went into the kitchen to pour the wine. While she was gone, Allen walked through the back gate and noticed Belinda. "Hi, I'm Allen, Crystal's brother. I don't think we've met. You must be Belinda, Crystal's landlord."

"Yes, I am. It's nice to finally meet you. I've heard so much about you," Belinda replied as Allen sat down beside her.

Seconds later, Nathan appeared in the upstairs back door. "Who are you and what are you doing here? Belinda, who is this man?" he snapped.

Allen was taken aback by the man's agitated entrance. "I'm Allen, Crystal's brother," he said quickly.

Nathan nodded curtly. "Belinda, come inside immediately," he said, disappearing into the house.

Belinda got up and started towards the door. "I'm so sorry. Tell Crystal I'm sorry about the wine. I'll see her some other time."

Crystal returned with the glass of wine and was surprised to see Allen sitting in Belinda's chair. "What happened to Belinda?"

"I'm not sure. I'll take the wine. Her husband came out and told her to go in. I must say he wasn't very friendly. He was pretty upset to find her out here talking to me. What's the scoop, do you know?"

"No, I don't. He just returned from Afghanistan the other night. I haven't met him yet. Belinda thinks he's different than when he left."

Crystal shifted in her chair, took a sip of wine, and looked at Allen. "I want to talk to you about a young couple at the diner, Netty and Max. She has fibromyalgia. I want to try to help them out if I can without it seeming like charity. I don't know much about them yet. They don't live far from the diner. They are a sweet couple who are too proud to take charity. I know what that's like. I thought between the two of us we could come up with something. I know she doesn't work and isn't able to outside of the home. I'm wondering if there's something she can do for Pearson from home. From what I know of the disorder, there are days she can't get out of bed. It would be wonderful if you could come up with an idea."

"I'll have to check with our human resources department and see what we can find for her. Leave it with me, and I'll let you know. What about Max? Do you know anything about him and if he works or anything?"

"No, I haven't been able to talk to them much, and I haven't asked a lot of questions. I don't want to scare them off. I'll try to get more information out of them periodically and let you know. In the meantime, I'd appreciate it if you might be able to find something for Netty."

"I'll look into it and get back to you. I'm going home. I told Maria I was coming here and wouldn't be long. I know she'll have dinner on the go."

Crystal smiled. "I'm so happy for you both. I can see such a change in you since the two of you moved in together. All the changes are for the better. Give her my love."

The next morning when Crystal arrived at the diner, Netty and Max were sitting in the corner booth. Crystal said, "Good morning," as she offered the coffee pot.

The two looked up and smiled. Netty was looking a bit more rested.

"You look better this morning. Were you able to get some rest yesterday?"

"Yes," Netty said, looking up at her with gratitude in her eyes. Max's hair was almost white, and his eyes looked almost gray. They showed signs of wisdom too extensive for such a young man. "You changed your hair colour," Crystal commented.

"Yeah, I do it often. It was time," Max replied.

This was a couple who knew all too well what tough times were. Crystal was hoping she could make a difference and help turn their lives around. "Max, do you work?" she asked.

"Yeah, I deliver parcels and letters for a courier company. It doesn't pay much, but it pays the rent and keeps food on the table. I'm hoping to be able to get something better down the road."

"I might know someone who can help you out if you're interested. My brother works for Pearson Computers. I could have him look into something for you if you'd like."

"Really? That would be cool! I would have to be able to keep the job I have now, though. Do you think that might be possible? I get a set rate and can depend on the money. I'd hate to lose the job I'm doing now. I work for Donavan Whitman. He doesn't like it when people quit and do other things."

"I'm not sure, Max. I don't understand why it would matter. I'm sure you'd do fine at Pearson. It wouldn't be a top job. At least, the pay and the hours would be better."

"Why don't we forget it?" Max replied quickly. "I'll keep doing what I'm doing until an opportunity comes up to move up while working for Donavan."

Crystal was confused by Max's answers. She turned towards Netty and asked, "Do you work, Netty? I'm sure with your condition it might be hard to hold down a full-time job."

"No, I don't work. There are days I can hardly get out of bed," she said half-heartedly.

"Do you use a computer?" Crystal asked.

"Yes, all the time. It passes the time for me when Max is out doing deliveries for Donavan."

"I could try to get you something with Pearson that you could do from home. Lots of people work from home on computers nowadays. Would you like me to ask my brother and see what he might be able to find you?"

Netty looked at Crystal with surprise. "You'd do that? If you could find me something that would be fantastic. It would make things so much easier for Max and me."

"Don't get too excited, Netty. You know people have made promises before that haven't come through," Max retorted.

"If there's something you can do for the company, Allen will find it for you. He's a great guy. You'd like him. I must get back to work before I have to start looking for another job myself," Crystal laughed.

Max looked up. "If your brother can find us jobs, why are you working as a waitress? Why aren't you working for Pearson Computers?"

"I did. In fact, when I started, I was in training for an executive position. I didn't like it. Then I went to work for a modeling agency run by Carlos Zambeni. I didn't like that either. I decided to go to work at what I know and try to figure out what I want to do from here."

"You worked for Carlos Zambeni, and you quit? He

mustn't have liked that!" Max exclaimed. "He's like Donavan when it comes to his employees. He has a reputation for not liking it when someone quits."

"I don't know whether he liked it or not. I figured if he needed to find me, he knew where to look. Sorry, guys, I must get back to work."

Crystal moved effortlessly around the diner taking orders, delivering food, and pouring coffee. She replayed the conversation with Netty and Max over in her mind. His reaction was confusing. Netty seemed all for the idea. Crystal did take note of the look Netty shot Max when the offer was made. Who was Donavan? Max had really sparked her curiosity with his reaction to her quitting her job with Carlos. She would have to ask Allen about it. He had been around Calgary and seemed to know everyone.

Crystal arrived home and heard shouting coming from upstairs as she entered her apartment. Belinda's husband was yelling, and Matthew was crying. Crystal was worried but decided to wait and see if it escalated before going upstairs to intervene. She wanted to make sure Belinda and Matthew were safe.

Crystal had seen on the news and read in the newspapers of the changed personalities that plagued soldiers when they returned from overseas. She was hoping this was not the case. She didn't know whether he'd been like this before he left or was starting to develop the personality changes she had heard about. She would have to keep an eye on Belinda and be alert for anything out of the ordinary. She turned on the television and started flipping through channels.

It wasn't long before the yelling stopped, and Crystal

heard the door slam and the car in the yard squeal out of the driveway. She turned the volume on the television down to listen. Matthew had stopped crying, and Crystal figured Belinda was putting him to bed.

Crystal picked up her glass of wine and could see Belinda sitting in her usual spot. Crystal opened the door and stepped out into the backyard.

"Hi. I thought I heard you come out. How are you?" she asked, trying to sound upbeat.

Belinda turned to look at Crystal as she sat down beside her. Crystal could see she had been crying.

"Are you okay?" Crystal asked sympathetically.

"I don't know what's going on," Belinda replied, as her emotions took over and she began to sob.

"Nathan is so angry. He was never like this. He lost his temper earlier over the most ridiculous thing. Matthew was crawling around the living room floor and knocked over a vase, and it smashed on the floor. Nathan turned around so fast and started yelling at me for not keeping an eye on him. Then he stormed out of the house and drove away. I'm not used to him being like this. It's like I'm walking on eggshells all the time. He gets so agitated and flies off the handle for no reason. It's hard now that Matthew is crawling. Nathan doesn't seem to have any interest in him whatsoever. It's like Nathan finds him more of a pain than anything. He should be thrilled to be able to spend time with his son, but it seems like it's the total opposite. I'm not sure what to do or think about it all. Tonight, he was very scary. I've never seen him like this.

Last night when he left, he went to the bar and came

home drunk. Nathan has always been a social drinker – you know, special occasions, sitting out here in the evenings, that kind of thing. But to go to a bar to sit and drink, he's never done that. He refuses to talk about it. As soon as I mention anything, he clams up and says nothing or tells me I'm imagining things and there's something wrong with me. I'm really starting to worry, Crystal. I don't know what to do," she said, as the tears flowed down her already tear-stained cheeks.

Crystal took Belinda's hand. "You should try to talk to someone at the base about what's going on at home."

"You're right. But I'm scared to. Nathan thinks seeking help from anyone for anything is a sign of weakness. He believes if we are strong enough to protect the country, then we are strong enough to deal with whatever is going on without anyone's help. He thinks it will hinder his career. I don't want to do that."

Crystal could see the turmoil her friend was going through with the recent changes in her husband's personality. "The way I see it, I'd be more worried about what's happening with him than hurting his career. You need to know if there's anything you can do to help him with the transition. There may be other women who are experiencing the same type of thing. They may have ideas on what to do or how to manage the changes he's going through. If the services are there, you should be using them."

Belinda looked at her, nodding her head. "I'll go tomorrow. Thanks, Crystal. It's nice to have you downstairs. I find you easy to talk to. How are things going at work? Anything interesting happening?"

"Things are going well, and I love my job. I've started talking to a young couple who are about my age. She has fibromyalgia and dresses completely in black. She's extremely attractive, even with all the black makeup and clothes. Her name is Netty. The boy that comes in with her is Max. His hair is dyed almost white. He dresses so differently. He's in baggy clothes and wears a backwards baseball cap. You know the look.

After I met them, I called Allen to see if I could find them work at the company. They look like they don't have a lot of money. I want to help them out with my connections if I can. I spoke to both of them about it today. Netty was all for it. I told her Allen might be able to find her something she could do from home on the days she couldn't get out of bed or outside. She seemed quite interested and pleased with the prospect.

Max's reaction, on the other hand, was very confusing to me. He's a delivery boy for Donavan somebody or other. He told me he wouldn't be able to quit his job to go work at Pearson because Donavan doesn't like it when people quit. I'm not sure what that's all about. I thought it would be something he would jump at."

"That does seem odd," Belinda replied, pondering Crystal's words. "You'll have to keep talking to them and see what you can find out. I do hope for their sake that Max changes his mind if they need the help you're trying to give them."

"All I can do is offer. If they don't take me up on it, I can't do anything about it. I'm going to talk to Allen, though, to see if he can shed any light on things for me. I won't see them for a few days. I'm working a different shift. We have a whole different crowd. I'm not sure I like it as much as the morning shift, even though I hate getting up early," Crystal laughed.

Belinda finished her wine, stood up, and stretched. "Speaking of getting up early, I'm going in. I don't know where Nathan has gone or when he'll be back, but I'm not going to wait up. Good night, Crystal."

"Good night, Belinda. I think I'll sit here for a while longer and enjoy the evening."

Crystal laid her head back against the chair and took a deep breath. Things were so different here in Alberta than what she had ever experienced before. She had lived in so many places, and yet every new one had its own personality.

Her childhood was like a road map. She'd visited so many little towns, dotting the Rand McNally, some of them not even big enough to garner a dot on the map. Yet, she'd thrived in all of them. She'd done well in school, despite being the new kid in the class four or five times in the same year. She was able to catch up to what they were teaching or was ahead of what they were doing, depending on where they were in the curriculum.

She'd found her high school days lonely. There were no parties, no close friends, no sleepovers or drive-in movies. She hadn't gone to the prom or had the opportunity to think about dating anyone. As an adult, she was starting over again living on her own. She liked it. No one recognized her anymore or asked her questions about her past. She was no longer the woman who had been found after twenty years of her parents' searching for her or thinking she may be dead. She was alive and doing well, and she liked how it made her feel. Yet, she couldn't forget Michael and Katie and their life in Corner Brook.

Chapter 14

MICHAEL SPENT THE NEXT FEW weeks working on business with Donavan. Allen was busy moving in with Maria and getting settled. Michael liked the changes he had seen in Allen since the move. He seemed more business-driven. He was drinking less and was more clearheaded.

Michael was busy putting the pieces of the investigation puzzle together. He knew he was getting closer to finding out who exactly Dreamweaver was. Donavan had opened up more about the underground area of his business.

He had arranged for Vinnie, a new line cook at Ruby's, to be there to watch Crystal and make sure she was safe. In that time, Vinnie had been paying attention to a relationship developing between Crystal and two young people who frequented the diner, Netty and Max. Michael investigated them and learned that Max was connected to Donavan. Max was a delivery boy for Donavan and was at his disposal.

Donavan liked the kid and gave him work to help support him and his girlfriend.

Michael attended social events when Donavan suggested he do so. He finally met Donavan's partner Carlos Zambeni. Donavan revealed that he and Carlos had been in business together for quite some time. They worked together often and always let the other know of any new and upcoming business opportunities. It was Donavan who'd suggested that Carlos start the modeling business.

Michael had done a solid background check on both Donavan and Carlos. The union was not recognized in the search. He would never have made the connection on his own. Michael started another full investigation into each of their backgrounds. He wanted to see when the union between the two of them took place. Once he had all the information he needed, Michael took an overnight flight from Calgary to Ottawa to discuss his findings with Ed and his superiors.

Michael sat in Ed's office going over the results of the investigation and the information he had gathered while working undercover in Calgary. He began telling them he suspected Donavan Whitman to be one of the largest suppliers of illegal drugs in the country, and suggested it was time to put an end to the organization.

"Ed, I believe Donavan is Dreamweaver and Carlos is his supplier for the Canadian market. It makes sense the way things are playing out. If we don't stop them now, we may never get another chance to get them," Michael said, looking at his friend across the desk.

"I agree with you, Michael. Where do you want to start?

Max may be a good place. He's young, and when he realizes where he'll spend the next twenty-five years, he'll roll. He and Netty would be put in the Witness Protection Program. It would be worth it to put Carlos and Donavan away for good. The program would relocate them and set them up with a whole new identity, jobs, and a house. They wouldn't be living hand to mouth the way they are now. You could go back to your life, hopefully with Crystal, and move forward. If we're going to do it, the time is now."

Ed and Michael met with Ed's superiors at the Canadian Secret Intelligence Service and told them of their plan. They were advised to go ahead. Michael flew back to Calgary the next morning without anyone knowing he had left the city.

Max continued to work for Donavan, and Netty was working from home doing research for Pearson Computers. They looked happier and healthier when they came in.

Crystal continued to encourage Belinda to go to the base. She had finally talked to a Peer Support Worker in their Operational Stress Injury Social Support Department. She learned that Nathan was suffering from post-traumatic stress disorder. He had been sent home because of the diagnosis. He was unable to perform his duties and had been placed on extended sick leave. Belinda was beginning to understand why Nathan was acting the way he was. She convinced Nathan to go for counselling with her to help them both cope with the changes in his personality.

The sessions were helping, and Belinda started to recognize when Nathan was experiencing an episode. This made it easier for her to manage her reaction to his behaviour. Nathan was working to reduce the effects of his PTSD, and

Crystal was happy for both of them. There were fewer fights upstairs, and Nathan started to join them in the backyard and showed much improvement.

Nathan was collaborating with base officials and was learning how to control his outbursts. He was working to help himself so he would not be released. He liked being in the military. It provided a good living for him and Belinda. His commanding officer was being patient while he attended counselling and could see he was working hard to keep his career intact.

Everything was going well for Crystal. She continued to talk to Gloria about Michael without any luck. He had completely disappeared, and if someone knew where he was, they weren't talking about why he'd left or if he was ever coming back. Crystal resigned herself to him being gone and settled into a nice routine between life and work.

Everyone in Ruby's Diner turned their heads as two police officers walked in and stopped in the doorway looking around. Netty and Max sat in the back corner hovering over their coffee and keeping their heads down. Max was always concerned wherever they went to keep from being noticed if they could. That's what they liked about Ruby's; it was not a hangout for law enforcement. Seeing police officers in the diner was not something that happened very often.

Crystal stepped forward to speak to the police, when suddenly, the door opened and in walked Michael with Ed at his side. She stopped short and couldn't believe her eyes. "What are you doing here? What are you doing in Calgary? Where's Katie? Is she all right?"

Michael walked up and leaned close to her ear. "I'll

explain later. For now, I've got a job to do. Once I've looked after what I've come to do, I'll be in touch."

Crystal nodded and watched as Michael and Ed made their way to the back of the diner to sit with Netty and Max. She knew by the look on their faces it was not good news. She hoped the kids were not in trouble. She knew Michael wouldn't be there unless it was serious. She went about her work and tried to concentrate on what she was doing instead of focusing on Michael sitting in the diner.

Netty and Max stood up and walked towards the door with Michael behind them. "Are they going to be, okay?" Crystal asked.

"That will depend," Michael said, ushering Netty and Max out the door and into the back of the police car waiting outside.

Michael and Ed spent the next couple of days talking to Max about Donavan and Carlos, and how involved he was with their organizations. Max was quick to hire a lawyer, who advised him to cooperate. His lawyer wanted him to make a deal with the police to save himself from spending an extended period of time in jail. Michael discussed the Witness Protection Program with their lawyer, and both Netty and Max agreed to the arrangement. They would be moved and given jobs to support themselves. It was a long way from how they had been living.

Michael was surprised at how much Max knew about the organization run by Donavan and his connection to Carlos. Max was cooperative after the police were arranging for him and Netty to go into witness protection. Max told Michael about how the drugs came into the country, who picked them up and how they were relayed throughout the city and across the country.

He revealed that Donavan and Carlos had been friends prior to striking up a business arrangement. Donavan had been the one who had set Carlos up when he arrived in Calgary and had helped him get the paperwork needed to live in Canada. Max believed the models for the agency owned by Carlos transported the drugs into the country. Some of them knew they were doing it and were well-paid, while others didn't. Max told Michael about the people Carlos had working for him and what happened when they didn't work out.

When Crystal told him about leaving Carlos to work in the diner, Max had been surprised he had let her go without any repercussions. Women didn't usually leave Carlos. Max thought Crystal being the daughter of Amanda Pearson might have had something to do with it. She was too high-profile as a lot of people knew who Crystal was. She was watched by the paparazzi, and Carlos didn't like them hanging around. Only when he was out to public functions showing himself in a good light did he want to be seen. At other times, he shied away and tried to avoid them.

Everyone was interested in him, who he was, where he came from and how he was quickly moving up the social ladder in the Calgary business world. There was a time when no one had ever heard of him. Now, he was invited to the best social events of the year and mingled with high-profile businesspeople. The paparazzi and the newspapers liked reporting on who he was, what he was doing and who he was doing it with, especially women. When he started dating Crystal, there had been a fair amount of speculation regarding their relationship and where it was leading.

Every girl he met wanted to be more than a business associate. That was what he liked about Crystal. She didn't have a clue who he was or anything about him. He had tired of her, though. She wasn't business-oriented and had a way about her that didn't fit into his plans or world. He had eased out of her life without making a scene about it since she was Amanda's daughter. The less press and media attention the whole thing received, the better for him.

Max confirmed he had heard the name "Dreamweaver" several times when he was working for Donavan. The name had been directed towards Donavan during those conversations. Max could testify to having knowledge of the inner workings of Donavan's underground operations. Max believed Donavan was the notorious Dreamweaver that CSIS was seeking and that he made all the decisions. He did consult Carlos, but not very often. Carlos was the shipping and receiving guy for the operation. They had limited contact with each other. They corresponded through letters in the drug packages. They did not have to meet, and correspondence between them was burned once it was read.

Max knew this because he had opened one of the packages he had picked up from Donavan before he delivered it. The package held a letter signed by Dreamweaver. Donavan didn't realize Max was watching from the shadows while he wrote the letter, signed it, put it in an envelope and dropped it in the package.

Max had opened the package and steamed open the envelope to read it before sealing it again and delivering the package. The delivery had been a bit late that day. Max covered his delay by saying there were problems on the city transit system. He assured Donavan it would never happen again, and it hadn't. Every delivery after that had been on time and without incident. That was why Donavan kept him on. He was dependable and made sure the deliveries were made, no matter what.

Michael asked Max to repeat what was in the letter. "I'm not sure who it was about. The letter was confirming arrangements for destroying a house by explosion owned by a CSIS officer. It was to be a warning. I overheard a conversation later stating that a woman and man had died. Donavan's only concern was with evidence left behind and that it couldn't be traced back to him. He was reassured there was none, so he was fine with the outcome. This was right after I started working for Donavan."

Michael sat back in his chair, stunned. He couldn't believe what he was hearing. Donavan had been responsible for the death of his wife and his partner. Donavan was Dreamweaver. They had the testimony of Max to prove it. Michael sighed a heavy sigh of relief. The whole ordeal was over with the testimony of this young man, whom Crystal had led him to.

Michael and Ed finished taking down Max's statement and told Max they were going to put him and Netty somewhere until the trial. Michael wanted to make sure they were safe before arresting Donavan and Carlos.

Michael called his mother and asked if he could send Netty and Max to Nova Scotia to stay until their future was secure. "Absolutely, you can. Send me the details, and I'll have one of the security guards pick them up at the airport.

I'm so glad this is finally coming to an end and you and Katie can move forward in your lives without Katrina's death hanging over your head. You can finally lay her to rest by putting the men responsible behind bars. Have you spoken to Crystal yet?" she asked.

"One step at a time, Mom," Michael replied. "I want to have this whole case over before doing that. Then I too can know it's over, and Crystal will have to make up her mind as to what she wants to do. I'll ask her when I'm finished if she'll come home with me. Who knows what she'll do? She hasn't done anything we've expected since I've met her. I'm not counting on anything."

"I guess you're smart, son. I only want to see you happy," Virginia said.

"It'll be over soon, Mom. I'll let you know when Netty and Max are going to arrive. Thanks for letting me send them there. I appreciate it."

"Don't think twice about it, Michael. I'll look forward to meeting them. I've got to get supper ready for Katie. I'll wait to hear from you."

"I'll be in touch soon. I love you, Mom," Michael said, hanging up the telephone.

Time sped by, and Michael could hardly keep up with everything that was happening. Donavan and Carlos were arrested and charged with numerous offenses. They were being held in jail pending a bail hearing. This gave Michael time to get Netty and Max out of the city and on their way to safety in Nova Scotia before Carlos and Donavan were back on the street. Their passports and assets were seized so they couldn't leave the country. They were also not allowed to leave the city limits. Michael assigned two plainclothes police officers to ensure they did not.

Netty and Max arrived at his mother's while arrangements were made for them to enter the Witness Protection Program and start their new lives. They were both excited about the possibilities their new life would hold. They would never have to worry about a place to live, food on the table or a job ever again.

Michael knew he couldn't avoid talking to Crystal any longer and picked up the phone to call her. She had been shocked to see him, and he hadn't spoken to her since he had escorted Netty and Max out of the diner. It was time to make the call and see where their relationship stood and if she wanted to come home.

He dialed the number and heard Crystal's voice say, "Hello?"

"Crystal? It's Michael. I'm calling to see if you want to get together for coffee, dinner or a drink while I'm in Calgary."

"Hi, Michael. Why don't you come over tomorrow night? I'll make dinner. Does seven o'clock work for you? I have to work the morning shift, but I'll be home early to mid-afternoon."

"Sounds great. I'll see you tomorrow night. Thank you, Crystal. I'll look forward to seeing you," Michael said and hung up the phone.

Crystal found it hard to concentrate at work the following day. Things had returned to normal at the diner after the gossip surrounding the police visit had died down. Netty and Max hadn't been back since they had left with Michael. Crystal was going to ask Michael when she saw him what had happened to them. They were good kids, and if they were in trouble, she hoped it was not too bad.

The news was filled with information on Donavan and Carlos, their arrest, and their connections to the underground drug trade. Crystal couldn't believe it. She had dated and traveled with Carlos. It made her sick to think he may have used her or anyone else to further his illegal drug importation. To think Max may have been tangled up in the whole mess was surprising to Crystal, and she worried about what might have happened to them. There hadn't been anything in the news regarding Netty and Max.

Crystal didn't say a word to anyone about her upcoming meeting with Michael and left the diner for home. She drove down Blackfoot Trail to her apartment in the southwest end. She stopped and picked up two porterhouse steaks and the ingredients for a salad. She dropped in to Willow Park for one of her favourite bottles of red wine. It came recommended by one of the staff. She was pulling on a clean t-shirt and jeans when the doorbell rang.

Crystal nervously opened the door. "Hi, Michael. Come in," she said, stepping aside so he could enter the tiny kitchen. She didn't want to get too excited about why he was there in case she was wrong. She hoped he would be asking her to go back to Corner Brook. It was hard to think that he might just be there for a visit.

"Hi, Crystal. It's good to see you," Michael said, stepping inside and closing the door. He could see she had changed. It was apparent living on her own had been good for her.

"Would you like a beer? I do have wine, and there's beer in the fridge."

"I'll have a beer. I can get it myself," Michael said, walking towards the fridge.

"I have a couple of steaks if you wouldn't mind barbecuing while I put together a salad."

"That sounds delicious, but I'd like to sit and talk to you. It's early, and there's so much I need to tell you," he said, taking her hand and looking her in the eyes.

"Okay, I'll pour myself a glass of wine, and we can sit and chat before dinner," Crystal replied and led him into the living room to sit beside her on the couch.

Michael started at the beginning. He answered a few questions when she asked for clarification. She mostly stayed quiet and listened closely to what he was saying. He explained his past, who he really was and what he had done prior to arriving at the police station in Corner Brook. He talked about his late wife, Katrina, what had happened the day of the explosion, and how she and his partner Brian had died. He told her how he blamed himself and how frustrated he had become when he couldn't find Dreamweaver. He described why he'd come to Calgary and how he had spent the last few months undercover trying to figure out if Donavan was Dreamweaver and trying to find evidence against Donavan and Carlos. He explained how he had bumped into Allen, and how despite the ongoing investigation he had really liked the time he had spent with him.

Crystal was surprised to learn he had followed her to Calgary to ensure her safety while he moved around the city gathering evidence on Carlos and Donavan. She laughed when she realized her Michael was the same Michael that Allen was trying to introduce her to. She listened as Michael told her about Netty and Max and where they were, along with Katie. He told her Katie was anxious to see her again and wanted to show her Midnight. She wanted to introduce Crystal to the friends she had made while staying with her grandmother. He let her know that he had been in touch with the police department in Corner Brook and was planning to return to his job. Gloria and Samuel knew of his return, and the only matter that needed to be clarified was whether she would be returning with him.

Michael dropped on one knee beside the chesterfield and pulled out the engagement ring his father had given his mother. "Crystal, I've been lost without you. Katie loves you and is hoping for me to bring you home. I want you to be my wife. I don't want to be without you ever again. Will you marry me?"

Crystal began to shake uncontrollably. "Of course I'll marry you, Michael. I love you. I don't want to be without you and Katie. I want to go home and back to our lives."

Michael slipped the little ring on her finger and sat next to her, taking her into his arms and kissing her passionately. "I love you, Crystal."

Michael went out into the backyard and started to barbecue as Crystal made the salad for dinner. Nathan came out and introduced himself. Crystal could see Michael and he were talking about something serious. Nathan shook Michael's hand and went back inside the house. "What was that all about?" Crystal asked as she came out to see if the steaks were done.

"Nathan wanted to know who I was and had a few questions for me about the police force. He may have to find another form of work. He was thinking with his military background that he would look into policing. He told me he is suffering from PTSD, and he may not be able to stay in the armed forces because he was no longer deployable. I told him there were many people suffering from the disorder and that he was not alone. I suggested a couple of support groups and places in the Calgary area that may be able to help him."

Crystal looked at Michael with love in her eyes. "They're such a wonderful couple. I've become quite attached to them, especial the little boy. He's such a sweetheart. Belinda and I have had some great chats in the backyard in the evenings. I'll miss them, even Nathan. He's not a bad guy when he isn't freaking out over something. He's a lot better since he stopped drinking and has been going for counseling. I do hope it all works out for them."

"If it's any consolation, I've told Nathan to let me know if he submits an application to the police force. I'll do what I can to help him once his PTSD is under control." Michael winked at her.

Crystal smiled and said, "Let's eat. It looks like the steaks are done."

The next week was a whirlwind for Crystal. She and Michael planned for one of Michael's colleagues to take over Crystal's lease with Belinda and Nathan. That way, Nathan would have someone downstairs who was familiar with PTSD and Belinda would have an in-house support system.

They dropped in to see her parents and visited with Allen and Maria. There were tears in her eyes as she said goodbye to Jonathan. Jonathan smiled and wished them both well. "I always said we should've left you where you were. Be happy, Crystal, and keep in touch."

"I will, Jonathan. I know in my heart that Newfoundland is where I belong. I'll never forget you and what you've tried to do for me. Please come and visit us when you can. We'd love to have you," Crystal said, giving him one last hug.

Amanda's reaction to her leaving and marrying Michael was not surprising. "I don't understand why you'd want to leave everything that is Pearson Computers to return to a little hick town in the middle of nowhere. But I'm not going to try to stop you. I've given it my best shot to keep you here in Calgary. If you ever change your mind, you're more than welcome to return. There will always be a place for you, Crystal. That's the least I can do."

"Thank you, Amanda. I'll never forget my time here. I've enjoyed getting to know you. It's good to know who I am and where I come from. I'm happy to be returning with Michael and Katie. Corner Brook is far from a hick town, and it represents the home and community I've always dreamed of living in. We can certainly visit back and forth whenever we want."

Crystal and Michael turned and walked towards the door. It was time for them to fly back to Nova Scotia, get Katie, and return to Newfoundland. The plane landed in Halifax, and Michael took the wheel of the rental as they drove away. As they travelled along the South Shore of Nova Scotia, they could smell the salt air and hear the seagulls shrieking. They hadn't told Katie or Virginia they were coming. They wanted it to be a surprise.

Katie was tying Midnight to the hitching post and

turned to see the car pull into the driveway. It took her a minute to recognize who was in the car. She started running towards it shouting, "Dad and Crystal are here! Dad and Crystal are here!"

Virginia came out onto the porch with Netty and Max close behind as Michael and Crystal stepped out of the vehicle. "It's about time you got here. We've been waiting to hear when you'd arrive," Virginia said, walking towards Michael to give him a hug. Virginia stepped back from Michael and turned towards Crystal. "You must be Crystal. I'm Virginia. Welcome. It's good to finally meet you."

Katie was all over Crystal and was so excited to see her. "I've missed you so much. I hope you're going to stay. Come see Midnight," she said, dragging Crystal towards the pony.

"As a matter of fact, I am. Your father has asked me to marry him, and I've said yes, if that's okay with you?"

"Are you kidding? That means you'll be my stepmother. I can't wait for that to happen."

Crystal played with Katie and spent time talking to Netty and Max before the security guards drove off with them to start their new lives. She was relieved to hear they would be looked after and was glad they were away from Calgary, Donavan, and Carlos. This would give them both a fresh start.

Crystal looked around and smiled at Michael, Katie, and Virginia as they all sat at the dining room table eating dinner that evening. She was where she wanted to be and knew she, Katie, and Michael would have a wonderful life together. She couldn't wait to get home to Corner Brook to see Gloria and Samuel.

Michael stood at the airport the next day and hugged his mother. There were tears in everyone's eyes. "Thanks, Mom, for everything. Take care of yourself and come visit us when you can."

"I will, Michael, but you know I don't like to leave the farm. I'm still leery about how far Dreamweaver can reach, even though he's in jail."

Michael smiled at his mother. "You don't have to worry about him ever again. He and Carlos are going away for an exceedingly long time. We're free to live our lives without worrying about what's going to happen."

"It's hard to believe it's finally over. It'll take some time for it to sink in. I'll visit sometime soon, I promise," Virginia said, relieved.

Michael hugged his mother again then turned towards Crystal and Katie, who were waiting to board the aircraft. "Let's go home," he said, taking Katie's hand and putting his arm around Crystal to walk through security to the gate.

Acknowledgements

I would like to acknowledge those who have supported and worked with me to create the stories I feel blessed to be able to put down on paper.

To Susan Tremills for doing the editing. I don't know what I would have done without your help in making this story happen.

To Rebecca and Nick, my children, who have been behind my writing efforts since day one, with a word of encouragement, and the patience to wait until such time as Mom was finished writing.

To Andrea, my sister. I don't think this book would have ever been finished had it not been for you. Thank you for reading the first few chapters and encouraging me to continue.

To all my Angels who support, guide and inspire me with stories, characters, and the ability to form sentences on even my worst writing days; without them, there would be no Angel Power.

COMING SPRING 2023

When Love Comes Knocking

By

Angel Power

Abigail Chase lived a quiet life on the farm with her
father Nathaniel. Until one day, while horseback riding,
she comes across a vacant cabin and has a run-in with a
stranger living alone, who changes her life forever.

About the Author

Angel Power is an Adventurer, former Event Coordinator and retired Truck Driver who has traveled extensively in Canada, the USA and Europe. She is the author of A Trucker Girl's Dream and has been published in numerous newspapers and magazines. She has worked with some of Canada's top professional entertainers and is a firm believer in living life to the fullest. When she's not working on a new novel, she spends her time traveling, horseback riding and hiking. You can find her on Facebook https://www.facebook.com/profile.php?id=100070679596920

CPSIA information can be obtained
at www.ICGtesting.com
Printed in the USA
BVHW070946010223
657353BV00001B/12